RESCUING
SENECA CRANE

RESCUING SENECA CRANE

Susan Runholt

VIKING

VIKING
Published by Penguin Group
Penguin Group (USA) Inc., 345 Hudson Street, New York, New York 10014, U.S.A.
Penguin Group (Canada), 90 Eglinton Avenue East, Suite 700, Toronto, Ontario, Canada
M4P 2Y3 (a division of Pearson Penguin Canada Inc.)
Penguin Books Ltd, 80 Strand, London WC2R 0RL, England
Penguin Ireland, 25 St Stephen's Green, Dublin 2, Ireland (a division of Penguin Books Ltd)
Penguin Group (Australia), 250 Camberwell Road, Camberwell, Victoria 3124, Australia
(a division of Pearson Australia Group Pty Ltd)
Penguin Books India Pvt Ltd, 11 Community Centre, Panchsheel Park, New Delhi – 110 017, India
Penguin Group (NZ), 67 Apollo Drive, Rosedale, North Shore 0745, New Zealand
(a division of Pearson New Zealand Ltd.)
Penguin Books (South Africa) (Pty) Ltd, 24 Sturdee Avenue, Rosebank, Johannesburg 2196, South Africa

Penguin Books Ltd, Registered Offices: 80 Strand, London WC2R 0RL, England

First published in 2009 by Viking, a member of Penguin Group (USA) Inc.

10 9 8 7 6 5 4 3 2 1

Copyright © Susan Runholt, 2009
All rights reserved

LIBRARY OF CONGRESS CATALOGING-IN-PUBLICATION DATA IS AVAILABLE
ISBN: 978-0-670-06291-1

Printed in USA   Set in CG Cloister

To the rest of my warm and wonderful
family, Rusty, Patty, Steve, and Robyn,
a built-in, four-person cheerleading squad,
marketing team, editorial board,
and support group.

Eternal gratitude for your love and friendship.

1
Prelude

The first time I saw Seneca Crane, she came onstage at a Minnesota Orchestra concert, sat down at the piano, and played a Mozart concerto. She got a standing ovation.

She was thirteen then, just a year older than I was. She was wearing a short, shimmery silver dress, and her hair was in cornrows and long braids.

I was sitting near the front with my mom and my best friend, Lucas (who's a girl), so we could see Seneca up close. She was pretty, with smooth skin a little darker than coffee ice cream, a cute little pointed chin, a small nose, and a long, graceful neck.

But when she came out and made that little bow musicians make before they play, what I mostly noticed were her eyes. They were big and dark and sparkly, the kind of eyes that show everything the person behind them is feeling. And just then, even though she was smiling, her eyes looked terrified.

While she played, those big eyes had a different expression: total concentration. She'd look at the keyboard, then at the conductor, who also would look at her to make sure she and the orchestra were perfectly together. For a while the two of them looked straight at each other, as if they were playing a duet or something. There was nothing scared about her now. She was in a whole different world, and you could tell she belonged there.

When she finished playing and everybody stood up and clapped, her eyes changed again. They lit up. In fact, her whole face lit up, as if to say, *I did it!* And her smile was nothing like the shaky one we'd seen before. This one showed bright, white teeth and big dimples. She looked incredibly cute. The audience loved her.

I remember at that time thinking I'd like to meet her, even though she was so pretty and so talented and I usually don't like people who are too perfect. But because of her eyes and how scared she looked before she played and how happy she was that she'd done a good job, I didn't envy her like I sometimes do with somebody like that.

In fact for some reason I felt a little bit sorry for her. Even then, before I knew anything else about her, I had the feeling she needed a friend.

Last fall, when she was fifteen and I was fourteen, I got to be her friend, and so did Lucas. We were in Scotland together, where she was scheduled to perform a bunch of concerts with an orchestra, and the three of us became really close.

And then something terrible happened to Seneca, and it was up to Lucas and me to help her.

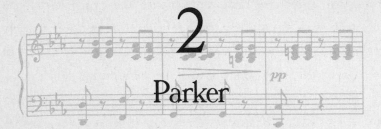

2

Parker

"You know when he misses me most, don't you?" Lucas said, in a whispery, dramatic kind of voice.

It was three o'clock in the afternoon on a Tuesday at the end of August. We'd just arrived by plane that morning in Edinburgh, Scotland, we'd had a nap, and now we were sitting at a sidewalk café outside our hotel in the middle of the amazingly huge Edinburgh Festival. The next day we were going to meet a world-famous teenage pianist. And what was Lucas thinking about? Josh Daniels.

Because even though this was the first thing she had said in the last twenty minutes, I knew it was Josh she was talking about. He was all she'd talked about for the last month.

I sighed. This was way more than I wanted to deal with on top of jet lag. But before I could say anything, she answered her own question. "It's when he gets to Café Olé."

She had her elbows on the table with her chin resting in both hands. Now she stared into space as if somewhere out there she could see Josh, sitting with the group of friends who always hung out together after school at their favorite coffee shop. From the look on her face, you knew that in her daydream Josh was missing her like crazy.

"I wonder if every afternoon, just for a moment, he forgets I'm gone. He laughs—he has that gift of laughter."

She always said that, and it always made me gag.

"Then he turns toward the door, expecting me to walk in. And suddenly"—she paused, and her voice dropped even lower—"he remembers."

This whole kind of thing makes me sick. It was all I could do not to say what I wanted to say, which was, *If he looks at the door and thinks of you, it's because he's so meeping glad you're not going to walk through it.* (*Meep* is a word Lucas and I use to substitute for the kind of words you can't say in front of most adults.)

It was in Café Olé that Lucas had met Josh. That was right after we got back from a summer trip to Amsterdam, and Lucas had fallen madly in love the minute she laid eyes on him. Josh had been just a little bit interested in her for about a week at the end of July. But it was obvious to me and probably everybody except Lucas herself that he couldn't care less about her now.

On her own, Lucas is one of the smartest, toughest kids I've ever known, boy or girl. In fact, my nickname for her is Lucas the Lionheart. She's a really strong person, and she doesn't take any meep from anybody.

But nobody's perfect, not even Lucas, and in her case the problem was guys. Well, actually, Josh—or, as I not-so-affectionately thought of him, Mr. Makes Me Want to Gag. She was obsessed with him. She not only thought he was still interested in her, she was sure he was the most wonderful human being who had ever walked the earth. And he definitely wasn't. He wasn't bad, but there was nothing special about him at all. He was just a cute guy who liked to play video games all the time—that is, when he wasn't at the coffee shop, flirting with all the girls and *talking* about video games. Mom once said he was "about as deep and interesting as your average mud puddle." What *did* Lucas see in him anyway?

Lucas hadn't wanted to go on this trip *at all* because she didn't want to leave Josh, but her other friends and Mom and I hoped that getting away for a couple weeks would help take her mind off him. Lucas's mother, Camellia, had wanted her to go, too, but I figured that didn't have anything to do with Josh. I thought it was because Lucas's dad was out of town working on a big legal case, Lucas's brother was at summer camp, and Camellia wanted to go up to stay for a week with some of her rich women friends on Madeline Island in Lake Superior. Camellia is always wanting to get her kids out of the way so she can do that kind of thing.

Anyway, I was the one who'd finally talked Lucas into going with us to Scotland by telling her that absence makes the heart grow fonder, and going to the world's biggest arts festival and hanging out around a famous musician would make her seem glamorous. Not even one day into the trip, stuck with Lucas all gaga, I was beginning to wonder what I had been thinking.

Personally, I was hoping we'd get into an adventure. Not as dangerous as the one we'd had in Amsterdam earlier in the summer, but enough to give Lucas something else to think about. I closed my eyes and said to myself, *Please, God, send us something exciting to take Lucas's mind off Josh Daniels*, not exactly meaning it as a prayer, but more as a way just to wish for something, if you know what I mean.

When I opened my eyes, I saw this, like, three-and-a-half-year-old kid with Asian features come toward me as fast as he could with his stubby little legs. He zigzagged through the sidewalk café tables, pulled up right in front of me, draped his arms over my lap, and said, "Are you the big girl who plays the piano?"

If somebody had told me this kid was the beginning of the adventure I'd just prayed for, there's no way I would have believed it.

Anyway, I looked at Lucas, then back at the kid, raised my eyebrows, and said, "Well, I'm *a* big girl, and *sometimes* I play the piano. . . ."

That wasn't good enough. He turned to Lucas. "Are *you* the big girl who plays the piano?"

"I'm the big girl who plays the violin," Lucas said.

By this time he was staring at Lucas, his eyes huge. "You have pink hair!" he said.

"It's red. Red hair. And it's only parts of it."

The kid had it right. It was pink. When Lucas first met Josh, he had orange streaks in his hair. So she'd gone to the drugstore, gotten some Manic Panic, and put red streaks in hers. This made her mother, who's, like, obsessed with looks and fashion, go ballistic. Anyway, now the dye had faded, and Lucas's hair was almost back to being its normal self, which is reddish blond and curly. But there was still a little pink in some of the streaks.

The kid said, "Can I touch it?"

"Sure, if you don't pull it."

"*Par-ker*! What are you doing?" came a woman's voice from a few yards away.

"She said I could touch her pink hair!"

"I'm sorry he's bothering you," the woman said, grabbing Parker and looking embarrassed. She was pretty, with long, light-brown hair that went all the way down her back. She stuck her free hand out to Lucas and smiled. "I'm Laura Weiss, and this is my son, Parker." I wondered if Parker was adopted or if his dad was Asian.

"It wasn't any bother. I'm Lucas Stickney, and this is my friend Kari Sundgren."

We finished shaking hands, and Laura said, "I think I saw you on the plane. Are you traveling with the orchestra?"

But before either of us could answer, Parker said, "My daddy plays the tim-pa-ni, and my mommy plays the oboe in Or-ches-tra Sifica," his way of saying *Orchestra Pacifica*.

"That's pretty cool, Parker," I said. "And what do you play?"

"Trucks."

When we all finished laughing, Lucas answered Laura's question. "We're traveling with Kari's mom, Gillian Welles. We're here so she can write a story about Seneca Crane for *Internationale* magazine, where she works." If you haven't heard of it, *Internationale* has articles about art and culture from all over the world, and Mom got a job there after she wrote a piece about that Amsterdam adventure I mentioned, when Lucas and I solved an international art crime. Mom has to travel a lot for her work. When we can, Lucas and I go with her.

"In fact," Lucas added, "Gillian is interviewing Seneca right now."

Parker piped up. "Seneca! *That's* the big girl who plays the piano!"

"Yes, Parker," Laura said, bending down to talk to him. "She's going to play the piano with the orchestra for some of our concerts. Now don't interrupt." She straightened again. "Are you guests here, at the hotel?"

"Yeah," I answered. "Mom wanted to stay where the orchestra's staying."

"Good. We'll look forward to seeing you around. It's been nice to meet you." Then came the inevitable question, aimed at both Lucas and me: "By the way, do you babysit?"

Lucas and I looked at each other. "Sure," I said.

"Great. I'll be in touch. Say good-bye, Parker."

The minute they were gone, Lucas settled in again with her chin on her hand. Fortunately, before she could say anything stupid, Mom showed up.

"Hi, guys," she said, plopping herself down in a chair. "Are you enjoying this sunshine?"

Lucas grunted. Mom, who was used to the Josh-obsessed Lucas by now, ignored her.

"I just got finished interviewing Seneca. Lovely young woman. I think the three of you will get along. Her mother and stepfather are very interesting," she added. Her tone of voice on the last part made me wonder what she meant.

"What are they like?" I asked.

Mom shook her head. "I'm not going to say any more right now. I'll let you make your own judgments."

She looked at another table, where the waiter was taking an order. "I wish he'd come over here. I'm dying for a cup of coffee." She turned back to us. "And I haven't seen a newspaper today. In fact, I think I'll go inside and get a

Herald Tribune so I can see what's going on in the world. When the waiter comes, could you order a caffè latte for me?" She got up as if to go.

"You stay here, Mom. I'll go in and get the paper for you," I said. It was a perfect opportunity to get away from Lucas's imaginary relationship with Mr. Makes Me Want to Gag.

Mom, who wasn't used to having me volunteer to do much of anything, looked at me like I was crazy, and I shot a glance toward Lucas.

"Ah," Mom said out loud, but Lucas didn't move a muscle. I think you could have fired a cannon in front of her, and she wouldn't have moved.

I took the coins Mom handed me and headed out of the sunshine and into the hotel lobby, where a little shop sold newspapers and magazines and candy and things. With the bazillion people who were in town for the festival, it was no surprise there was a huge line at this place. That wasn't all bad. More time away from Lucas. I grabbed a copy of the *International Herald Tribune* from a stack and got in line.

I ended up next to a big inside window between the lobby and the hotel's coffee shop, where we'd eaten breakfast that morning. Beyond the glass, just feet away from where I stood, a guy was sitting at a table with his back to me, trying to make a call on his cell phone. I saw him punch in numbers, then put the phone up to his ear. Something must have gone wrong, because a second later he pulled the phone away, stabbed at what must have been the off button, looked down at what I figured was a phone number, and started punching numbers again.

That didn't seem to work either. When it didn't work the third time, he snapped the phone shut and banged it down on the table so hard that I could hear the smack all the way out to where I stood. The next thing I knew, he'd come up to talk to a clerk sitting behind a desk near me in the hotel lobby.

The angry guy had his back to me, so I couldn't hear what he said, but when he finished, I heard the hotel clerk say, "I'm sorry you're having a problem, sir. Where are you calling, if I may ask?"

The angry guy said something, and the clerk repeated it, but I wasn't sure what it was. In Scotland they speak English, but their accent—what Mom calls a burr—has different sounds for some letters and lots of rolled *r*'s, and it can be hard for an American to understand. This word sounded something like *poor tree* or *poetry*. Anyway, the clerk replied, "To call that area you have to precede the number written on your paper with these digits," and he wrote something down.

The angry guy turned away from the desk and, his back still toward me, walked out the front door of the hotel, punching the buttons on his phone. He didn't even say thank you. What a jerk!

After I paid for the newspaper, I went back outside

and waited for a break in the crowd of people passing on the sidewalk. Edinburgh is a super-old city with really beautiful buildings. Our hotel was on a busy corner on the Royal Mile, which is a street that runs right through the middle of the oldest part of town. At one end of the street is this palace called Holyroodhouse where the queen of England—or, as the Scots say, the queen of Great Britain—sometimes stays. At the other end, almost exactly a mile away, is Edinburgh Castle, a huge medieval fortress surrounded by tall, dark-gray stone walls. Now, during Festival—we already figured out that that's what the locals call it—the Royal Mile and the areas around it were the most crowded of any place in town. And our hotel was on a corner where the Royal Mile intersected with a street that led over this long bridge with a ton of traffic, so it was especially busy.

As I waited to get into the traffic and snake through to our table, I could see Mom sitting with her coffee in her hands, looking out at the people going by and smiling. Lucas was staring out in the same direction Mom was, but I was pretty sure she wasn't seeing the streets or the sunshine or the crowd. She had this spaced-out look in her eyes and a little smile on her face, which might have been jet lag, but probably meant she was having some nauseating daydream that could have come out of a cheesy romance novel starring her and Mr. Makes Me Want to Gag. Of course she'd want to share it with me, and of course I would listen. She *is* my best friend, after all, and we're there for each other in the good, the bad, and the crazy times.

Still, friend or no friend, I had to take a deep breath just to get the strength to keep walking toward them. I love traveling, I already loved Edinburgh, and I was looking forward to spending more time here and in other parts of Scotland. But in spite of all of that, I was dreading the next two weeks.

Hearing about Josh meeping Daniels had gotten seriously old.

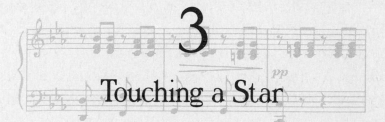

3
Touching a Star

The next morning, Mom, Lucas, and I walked down the street from our hotel and across the bridge I told you about. Then we turned onto another big Edinburgh street, called Princes Street, heading for the Usher Hall, where Seneca would be rehearsing with the orchestra. Every day during Festival there are more than a thousand theater and dance and music performances going on, and more than a million people come to town during the three weeks to be part of the festival crowd. Edinburgh isn't a really big city (it's only about the size of Saint Paul, Minnesota, where I come from, if you count our suburbs), and the shows take up every possible place in town—every school, every church, every banquet room, every place a club would meet, even some bars and restaurants. Like I said, everywhere. In all the busiest parts of town there are performers on the sidewalks doing pieces of their acts to try to get you to come and see their shows. Some of the festival artists only perform outside and put out a basket or instrument case or something where people can throw in money.

All the way along the first half of Princes Street, there were these outside entertainers. Just on that one walk we saw two different guys dressed in kilts and big furry hats playing bagpipes, a jazz trumpeter who was really good, a juggler, a magician, and a guy who balanced an entire bicycle on his nose. An entire bicycle. I am not making this up.

When we got to the Usher Hall, we saw a mini billboard for the Orchestra Pacifica concerts. The orchestra's new conductor was a Scot who had conducted an orchestra in Scotland so that's why they'd been asked to play at the festival. They were performing on seven nights over two weeks. Seneca Crane was the guest artist for three of the concerts. The artist for the other four concerts was a violinist.

The Usher Hall is built in a circle, and we had to walk around to the back of it off a side street to get to the stage door, where the guard let us in. Once we were inside, the guard talked into a little microphone on his desk, then asked us to wait until somebody came to meet us.

While we stood there, we could hear the sound of scales being played on a piano from somewhere in the distance. In a minute we saw a good-looking man coming down the hall toward us. He gave us a big smile with lots of even white teeth, then turned toward Mom. "Gillian," he said, and touched Mom on the arm, "*so* good to see you again."

For a guy his age, he was really hot: tall; slender, but with lots of muscles; that big, white smile; dark brown hair and dark eyes. I noticed he was wearing a lot of men's cologne. It made me want to breathe through my mouth.

"Paul, I'd like you to meet my daughter, Kari Sundgren, and her friend Lucas Stickney," Mom said, ignoring the whole so-good-to-see-you business. "Girls, this is Mr. Didier, Seneca's stepfather."

"Kari," he said, taking my hand in both of his. Then he looked right into my eyes for a second, and I had the feeling he was really paying attention to me. "You look just like your lovely mother."

Mom is kind of tall and has green eyes and naturally curly black hair. It may have a little gray in it, but Mom always takes care of that. I do look like her, only I'm shorter, my hair isn't quite as curly (and doesn't have any gray in it, of course), and my eyes are more hazel than green.

"A lot of people say that," I said.

"I'm sure they do." He was still looking into my eyes and smiling. "The resemblance is remarkable.

"And Lucas," he said, turning toward her. "How did you manage to get hooked up with these two?" He gestured toward us with a movement of his head and a friendly smile as he took her hand and looked into her eyes.

"Kari and I have been best friends since fifth grade, Mr. Didier," Lucas said. "I usually come with them when they travel."

"It sounds fortunate for everyone. Please, all of you, call me Paul. Seneca's practicing on the main stage. It's this way." And he started off, leading us down the hall, which was crammed with instrument cases and all kinds of crates from small to huge, all the way around to the other side of the building.

It wasn't until I saw the back of his head that I realized I'd seen this guy before. This was the same guy who'd been trying to make that telephone call in the hotel. I was sure of it.

When Paul's back was turned, Mom looked at us and raised her eyebrows, and I remembered what she'd said about Seneca's mom and stepfather being *interesting*. Either she was impressed by the guy's charm or, more likely for Mom, she thought it was a little too much. I was dying to tell her about Paul and the cell phone.

"We're all delighted to have you along," Paul was saying. "This is Seneca's first international appearance with an orchestra, and she's under a lot of pressure. Of course, she'll have to focus on rehearsals and performances much of the time, but we think being with people her age whenever she's free will help relieve her stress."

We walked to a door where the sound was coming from. Now Paul put his fingers to his lips and slowly pulled the door open into the audience section. He gestured to a row, and we scooted in and sat down.

On the stage in front of us was Seneca Crane, playing scales on a grand piano.

She looked so different from her surroundings that it was almost funny. There she was, this little person dressed in capri jeans, cool canvas shoes, and a T-shirt, surrounded by this big, fancy hall all decorated in white and gold.

She looked way different from when I'd seen her in Saint Paul two years before. For one thing, she'd cut her hair, and now it was spiked out. But one thing was the same: that total concentration on what she was doing. She was playing scales in a way I'd never played them for my piano lessons. She'd start with a few notes with her right hand, then begin the same scale with her left hand, as if it was a round, like "Row, Row, Row Your Boat," where singers come in at different times with the same song. She went up so quickly it was like a wave going over the notes, octave after octave, then down again, never missing a note. She just kept doing it, changing from one key to another, making what I knew was very hard look very easy.

Paul, who was leaning over next to us, glanced down toward a woman sitting in the very first row of seats. "I'll go and sit by my wife now," he whispered, making almost no noise. "Seneca's been doing her technical work for"—he looked at his watch—"almost forty-five minutes, so she'll be starting the music any time. Gillian, yesterday you said you had some questions for Seneca's mother and me. Would you all like to join us for lunch after the rehearsal?"

Mom nodded and smiled, and Paul went down to join his wife. When he sat down, he leaned close to whisper something to her, and she turned toward us. She and Seneca looked a lot alike, but although Seneca was at least part African American, this woman, her mom, had light skin, and her long hair was dark brown instead of black. I had thought of Seneca as pretty, but I could see that if she grew up to look like her mother, she was going to be beautiful.

After only a glance at us, the woman turned back around and said to Seneca, "Maybe we should get started on the Gershwin."

Seneca didn't say a thing, just kept her eyes on the keyboard, as if waiting for directions.

There was another little conference between Paul and Seneca's mom, who then looked back up at the stage and said, "Sorry, darling. What do *you* want to start with?"

"Um, could I just warm up with the Chopin?" she asked in a timid voice.

"The Chopin first?!" her mom said, as if she was surprised and a little annoyed. Paul turned toward her, and she said, "Okay, go ahead."

Then it started, this beautiful music coming out of Seneca's fingers. It was a wonderful melody, like a love theme from a sad movie. She played it so well it sounded like a CD.

It only lasted a minute. When it was over, Seneca said, "Now I think I'm ready for the Gershwin."

The music started again. It took a few seconds before I recognized the piece, mostly because she was doing just her part on the piano, without the orchestra to play *their* part. Then suddenly I knew what it was. I'd heard it a lot when Mom listened to the classical music station. It was kind of half classical music, half jazz.

I breathed into Mom's ear, "What's this piece called?"

"*Rhapsody in Blue* by George Gershwin," she mouthed.

I loved it. I almost couldn't believe that somebody only fifteen years old could play like that, without ever making a mistake. So much feeling. So loud. So many notes!

When it was over, Paul and Seneca's mom started clapping. We joined in, clapping as hard as we could. There was somebody else clapping, too, a woman sitting behind us, smack in the middle of the main floor of the audience section.

"What did you think, Edie?" Paul, on his feet now, called out to her.

"Wonderful energy!" the woman shouted back. Even in the huge auditorium, her voice was a little too loud.

Paul turned to look at Seneca. "Seneca, you're gonna knock the festival audience dead."

Seneca showed her dimples.

"Didn't you think so?" Paul said in our direction, a big smile in his voice.

"I'm no music critic," Mom said, "but I thought it was a superb performance. Truly."

"What did you two think?" Paul called back to us.

"I wish I could play like that," I said, and Lucas said, "It was awesome."

"Come down here. I'd like you to meet everybody, Seneca," he said, and Seneca got off her piano bench and jumped down from the stage. The woman sitting behind us was coming up front, too, taking big steps, her head held high, as if she wanted to show how important she was.

Seneca's mom turned toward us. She was shorter than I'd expected, slender, and she wore tight jeans and a skinny top with a scarf looped around her neck. Very trendy. She was just as beautiful up close as she was from farther away, but when she looked at us, her brown eyes didn't seem friendly, and there was something about her mouth that made me think she was in a bad mood a lot of the time.

When we were all at the front of the stage, Paul said who we were, then, "This is my wife, Teresa Crane Didier, and"—gesturing to the other woman—"this is Edie Francis, Seneca's tutor. And this, of course, is Seneca."

The people with Seneca must have been used to having her be the star attraction, because they let her talk first. "I'm *so* glad to meet you," she said softly as she shook our hands.

It was weird finally being right there with her. Some-how, because I'd only seen her onstage, I had the impression that she'd be different from other people. Taller, maybe, or made out of something besides regular skin and hair and bones. But up close she was just like any other teenager, except she seemed more grownup.

Edie, on the other hand, was very tall. She wore a black pantsuit and black stiletto heels, which made her even taller than Mom. She was probably a little younger than Paul and Teresa, and very thin. She had a nose that was thin, too, a chin that stuck out just a little more than it should have, blonde hair cut shorter in back than in front, and brown eyes that didn't seem to show any feeling. She clasped a notebook next to her with her left arm.

"*Delighted* to meet you," she said—her voice was too loud again, as if she thought we were all hard of hearing—and shook Mom's hand.

Paul turned toward Seneca. "I was telling Gillian and the girls how much we're looking forward to having somebody besides just boring adults for *you* to hang out with."

Seneca smiled at us, and I was pretty sure she actually *was* looking forward to it.

Seneca's mother said, "Yes, we're very pleased," but I wondered if she was only saying it to make Paul happy. Already, just from the way she looked at him, I could tell she was really crazy about him.

"There are always a great many hours to fill on a tour of this sort," Edie said. She held her chin so far up in the air that she ended up looking down her nose at everyone.

"We trust you and Seneca will find pleasant ways to pass the time together."

I wanted to say, "Thank you, we will," in a voice as loud as hers, but Mom would've killed me.

Then Seneca had to start rehearsing again. The rest of us went and sat in the audience section, Paul and Teresa up close, the rest of us back in the middle with Edie.

Seneca kept working on *Rhapsody in Blue* for what seemed like forever, doing exactly what her mom told her to do, playing certain parts over and over until I was totally bored. We'd been sitting there for what seemed like an hour when Mom whispered something to Edie, then turned back to us and mouthed, "Women's room?"

Lucas and I nodded.

I'd put my backpack on the seat beside me, so I turned to pick it up. And that's when I saw the flash of green in the balcony.

4
The Mysterious Shape

At first it was just what you might call an impression, a kind of a flickering at the edge of the sunshine coming through one of the windows up there. But when I glanced to where I'd seen it, at the very farthest corner of the top of the two balconies, it turned out to be what might have been the shape of a man in a green shirt. Or maybe it was just a reflection. Whatever it was, it was there one minute and gone the next.

When I looked around, Mom and Edie were standing in the aisle while Lucas, in front of me, scooted down the row toward them. No one else had seen him or it or whatever it was. Nobody except me had even looked up.

I wanted to say something, but with Seneca playing I knew I'd get into trouble if I even whispered, so I caught up and followed the others out of the auditorium, my heart pounding.

I took a big breath of relief when we got into the corridor and the door closed behind us. "I think I just—" I said, starting to tell Lucas about it, when at the same time she mouthed to me, "I don't like that woman," and shot a look toward Edie, who was taking huge strides down the hall as if she felt important being able to show other people what to do, even if it was just to help them find the restroom.

I almost ignored Lucas and went on with what I was going to say, but it suddenly hit me that for once she was actually talking about something besides you-know-who. So I took another deep breath, which helped calm me down, and let her say whatever she wanted.

Mom and Edie were chatting away in front of us, and Lucas slowed down so she could whisper to me without their hearing. "Did you notice how weird her little speech was back there? 'We trust you'll find pleasant ways to pass the time,'" she said, imitating Edie's snotty voice. "It was like she was saying it that way on purpose, so it would look good if your mom wrote it down."

Just then we heard Edie give out this loud, fakey laugh at something Mom had said.

"Hark, I hear a giant sucking sound," Lucas muttered.

"Lucas, not to change the subject, but I think I saw something back there. In the balcony."

"Animal, vegetable, or mineral?" Lucas asked. She

didn't say it in a nasty way, but by this time she was opening the door to the women's room, so I let the subject
drop.

When we got back to our seats, I glanced up at the
balcony, but there was nobody there. For a while I tried to
figure out what I had seen. Had it actually been a person,
or had it been nothing but a flicker of green light?

The more I thought about it, the surer I was that whatever I had seen, it wasn't an actual human being. I was
trying to make a big deal about this because I wanted an
adventure.

I sighed and went back to listening to the music.

5

The Famous Pianist at McDonald's

"We came expecting Edinburgh's typical overcast skies, and instead, for the second day in a row, we have bright sunshine," Paul said, as we left the Usher Hall. "How about if we grab one of those outdoor tables before it's taken?" He gestured to an eating area outside the pub next door.

I pulled at Mom's arm and whispered, "Do you have questions to ask Seneca, or could Lucas and I take her to McDonald's?"

"McDonald's is fine as far as I'm concerned. But you'll have to ask Paul and Teresa," she said.

I gave her a dirty look, but I went ahead.

I always get nervous talking to grownups I don't know, and I ended up stumbling a little. "Um, there's this McDonald's we passed on Princes Street, and, um, I was wondering if Lucas and Seneca and I could eat lunch there." I turned to Seneca, "If you'd like to, that is."

Seneca's eyes lit up right away, but then she got a worried look and turned to her mother. Teresa was wearing dark glasses, so I couldn't see her eyes, but I had a feeling that she was glaring at me. "I'm not sure Seneca should be eating that. . . ." She stopped, looked at Paul, and said, "What do *you* think?"

"I don't see why not," he said. "Fast food once in a while won't kill her."

Seneca's mom shrugged. "Okay, I suppose so." Then she heaved this big sigh. Like Lucas had said, Edie wasn't the greatest, but I thought Seneca's mom was no prize either.

"When do we have to be back?" Lucas asked. "Maybe when we get done eating, we could take a little walk down Princes Street and see some of the outdoor artists. Have you seen any of them yet, Seneca?"

Seneca shook her head.

Teresa looked at Paul, and Paul looked at Edie. "Would you mind if Seneca was a half hour late for her lessons?" he asked.

Edie, chin in the air, said, "No, that's fine, Paul. We can get started at two thirty."

Paul turned to us. "I'm sure she'd have a great time. She hasn't seen much of the festival. We'll meet you back in our suite at the hotel at two thirty sharp."

I noticed the grateful look Seneca gave him just as Mom was handing us the money. And the next minute, the three of us were off on our own.

I've noticed that when teenagers get to know each other, we first have to pretend we have these great lives, everything's fine, we're so cool, etcetera, etcetera. But then when we get to be friends, the real truth starts to come out. I think deep down most of us feel we're not as great as we want people to think we are, but you usually have to get to know somebody pretty well before you start talking about that, or about other problems.

So I figured, with this glamorous career full of travel and being a famous piano prodigy and everything, Seneca would probably start out trying to convince us that she lived a perfect life. Then, when we got to know her better, we'd find out that underneath she was just like Lucas and me. But we hadn't been on our own for very long before I realized that I had gotten both things wrong.

When we'd lost sight of the grownups and were waiting to cross the street, Seneca said, "I can't believe my mother gave me permission to go to a fast food place. She's terribly strict about what I eat."

"What do you mean? You don't ever go to McDonald's or Burger King?" I asked as the pedestrian light turned green.

"I go with my cousin LaToya when I'm staying with her in the summer. I always stay with her for a week every year. She lives in Atlanta."

"But the rest of the year you never eat fast food?" I was trying not to sound as surprised as I felt.

"No. When I'm home in New York City or we're on the road with my music, Mom—" She broke off, and instead finished, "No, never."

Lucas said, "How about your stepdad? He doesn't seem so strict."

Seneca was quiet for a second. "He's trying to influence my mother to let me do more things."

"That's nice of him," Lucas said.

"Yeah," she said, and seemed to hesitate before she added, "everybody likes him."

I wasn't sure about her tone of voice. And as we walked toward McDonald's, I thought about what I'd seen the day before. I doubted if *everybody* liked him, but I decided not to say anything about Paul's cell phone tantrum until I was alone with Mom and Lucas.

The place was packed like everywhere else in Edinburgh during Festival. We got in line and I held up the money Mom had given me. "Mom said I should treat. What do you want to have, Seneca?"

"Maybe just a hamburger and a Coke?" It was a question, as if she was saying, "Is that an okay thing?" She sounded so timid.

"How about fries?" Lucas asked. At most places in Britain they called fries *chips,* but at McDonald's they were still called fries, just like at home.

"Sure."

We all ordered burgers and Cokes and got a couple of

orders of fries to split and one Dairy Milk McFlurry just to try it.

When we were sitting down and everybody had what they ordered, I said, "How do you like Edinburgh?" It wasn't very original, but it was all I could think of to say.

"It's wonderful!" Seneca said, and her eyes lit up. "My Grandfather MacIntosh, my mother's father, was from Scotland. He's dead now, but he used to talk about Scotland all the time. I always wanted to come here. I really like it." She stuck her straw into her Coke and took a sip.

"So, how is it being on this concert tour?" I asked.

She straightened, and her expression changed. "It's challenging, of course. Stressful," she answered in a confident tone of voice. "But it's the next artistic step for me, and I'm feeling ready professionally. The orchestra is going to be touring Europe for another two weeks after they leave Edinburgh. I wanted to make some appearances with them on that part of the tour. Mom and Paul thought that would be too much for me. But the really cool thing is that the orchestra is going to make a final appearance at Carnegie Hall in New York on their way back home, and I'm going to be the guest artist. I don't know if you know this, but a Carnegie Hall appearance is an enormous credential for a concert performer." She leaned back in her chair and right then, without her dimples, she looked exactly like what I thought a rock star or movie star would look like talking about her career.

I couldn't believe it. It was like Seneca had become a whole different person. Ten minutes ago she'd been sounding like a kid, younger than Lucas and I were, telling us about her mother being so strict, and not being able to go to McDonald's. Now here she was, looking and sounding like a celebrity in her twenties, and I was feeling nervous being around her.

She talked like that for a few more minutes, telling us about how the tour and the Carnegie Hall appearance would lead to more important (she used the word *prestigious*) concerts and higher fees for her appearances. Then she turned her head, sighed, and said, "Sometimes I wish I could just go to school like a normal person."

"Is Edie your only tutor?" I asked. "I mean, does she teach you all your subjects?"

She washed her bite of burger down with a sip of Coke and said, "Yes, she's the only one. It's too boring to talk about. Tell me about your school, and your classes."

Lucas and I were a little ahead of her in eating because she'd been doing most of the talking. So the two of us stuck our straws in the McFlurry, took sips, then launched into a description of our lives. We told her about the differences between my public school and the private school Lucas goes to, and about what classes we took.

All this time, Seneca was acting like she'd never heard anything so interesting in her whole life. Here she was, a famous pianist, and here we were, just regular kids going into ninth grade. But instead of us listening to *her* talk about places she'd been, and being on TV and everything, she was listening to *us* talk about American history and English classes.

Somehow in the middle of talking about school, Lucas managed to slip in something about Café Olé. *Uh-oh, here it comes,* I thought. By this time we'd finished all our food, so I said, "Those people standing with their trays look like they want our table. How about we head down Princes Street?"

I hoped this was going to keep Lucas from talking about Josh. I should have known better.

6

The Two Men in the Crowd, and the Schedule of a Pianist

Unfortunately, there weren't very many people performing outside on this end of the street, so in spite of the fact that there were lots of cool shops to look into and we even passed an outdoor market taking up one whole side street, there was nothing to keep Lucas from telling Seneca all about Josh. At least her version. I wanted to point my finger into my mouth, but stopped myself.

To get to our hotel, you had to walk a mile along Princes Street, then take a right and cross the bridge. I figured if Lucas had her way, we'd go directly there without stopping anywhere and just sit in the lobby until two thirty while she talked about Josh the whole time.

Seneca would probably have listened like she was in a trance, but I couldn't take it. So when we got to a big intersection, I led the way across the street to this enormous square in front of two museums, where we'd seen the guy balancing the bicycle on his nose. He was gone. An audience had gathered around a new act, and everybody was laughing.

Up ahead, standing on a little stage, were a big guy and a smaller guy wearing tweed jackets and kilts.

"Hey, it's a couple of Scottish comedians!" I said over my shoulder, and walked into the crowd.

Lucas shot me a look that said she wasn't exactly pleased to be interrupted. But Seneca's eyes were shining.

I wanted her to have a good time, so I was a lot less polite than I usually am, and was almost pushy getting us to a place at the very front, right at the edge of the stage, where we could see everything.

The comedians—they called each other Scotty and Scotty—were good, talking about Scotland's history and being Scottish in a really funny way. It was a little hard to understand them because they had big Scottish accents, and used different words, like saying *aye* instead of *yes*, and *lass* or *lassie* instead of *girl*, and *bonnie* instead of *pretty*.

The stage was totally surrounded by maybe two or three hundred people. After I'd watched the comedians for a while, I started looking around at the crowd—the young guy who couldn't keep his hands off his girlfriend, the couple looking perfect in their casual clothes and sunglasses, a group of older tourists who all seemed to be wearing sweatshirts and athletic shoes.

On the opposite side of the stage from me I noticed

two men who seemed to be watching *us*. As soon as they saw me glance at them, they both quickly looked back up at the stage.

One of the guys was tall, with black hair and a dark mustache. The other one, whose head was covered in stubble, wore a green-and-white striped soccer shirt with the word *Carling* on it.

A few minutes later, it happened again. I had that feeling people have when somebody's looking at them, and I glanced over at the skinhead and the guy with the mustache. Sure enough, there they were looking in our direction like before. Except by this time, somebody from behind us had pushed in between Seneca and me, so I could tell that the guys weren't looking at me, they were looking at Seneca, who was concentrating completely on the comedians and didn't notice the men watching her at all.

After they'd been staring at Seneca for what seemed like a long time, the skinhead said something to the one with the mustache, and the two gave each other a look and a kind of snickering smile. I wondered if they recognized her as a famous pianist, but that seemed odd—I'd been to enough concerts to know that these were not exactly the kind of guys who looked like they'd be fans of classical music. If they weren't music fans, why were they watching her?

I thought about that for a minute, then turned back to the stage and shook myself. This was the second time in the past few hours I'd gotten all suspicious over what was probably nothing.

· By this time, Scotty and Scotty were making jokes about somebody called Bonnie Prince Charlie, who I guess led this bunch of Highlanders in fighting against the English to get freedom for Scotland. Anyway, the smaller of the two Scottys would say something about how brave Bonnie Prince Charlie was or what a great leader he was. And every time he said one of these things, the bigger Scotty would say something insulting, like, "If he was so great, then why is Scotland still part of Great Britain? My sister has a pet Chihuahua who could have come up with a better battle plan than Bonnie Prince Charlie."

At some point in all of this, I looked back over for the two guys who'd been staring at Seneca, but they'd left or disappeared into the crowd or something.

Scotty and Scotty ended up by telling us that a real Scotsman doesn't wear anything under his kilt. That sounded pretty interesting. There were lots of men walking around Edinburgh in kilts. I figured I'd have to start looking at them in a whole new way.

When the show was over, I think Seneca clapped more than anybody. "That was awesome!" she said as we started back to the hotel.

"They were pretty funny," I said.

"What I liked was how much I found out about Scotland and Scottish people. Grandfather MacIntosh would have loved it. Hey, listen. It's 'Scotland the Brave'!"

The piper standing at the corner up ahead had just started playing a tune that I'd heard on the bagpipes about a hundred times since we got to Edinburgh. We got up in front of him and listened to it all the way through. He was really good, and when he was done, we tossed some money into the basket on the ground beside him.

As we left, Seneca said, "If Scotland were an independent country instead of part of Great Britain, 'Scotland the Brave' would probably be its national anthem. When my grandfather was alive, he told me that from ancient times there was a tradition that when Scottish soldiers went into battle, they'd all wear their kilts and somebody would lead the way playing the bagpipes. The soldiers had a reputation for being fearless. What was especially cool was that in World War I, the sound of the bagpipes and the sight of men in kilts was so weird and scary that the Scottish troops terrified the enemy, especially if it was foggy or getting dark or something. The Germans they were fighting called the Scottish soldiers the 'Ladies from Hell' or the 'Devils in Skirts.' Isn't that awesome?"

"That is seriously awesome," I said. "You're way into being part Scottish, aren't you?"

"Just call me Scotty," she said, and added, "although I might *look* a little different from most of the people who could have Scotty for a nickname." And with that she flashed a huge smile.

Both Lucas and I laughed. Of course, with her African American skin and hair, she didn't look at all Scottish. It was nice to see her sense of humor come out.

Lucas asked, "If you're part Scottish and part African American, how'd you get the name Seneca?"

"I'm a little bit American Indian, too. Seneca nation."

I've always thought it was kind of a cool thing about America that we can come from so many different races and nationalities. I would have said something about that, but just then the crowd of people on the sidewalk got so thick we had to fight our way through, and there was no way we could talk.

The sidewalk stayed packed like that all the way up to the bridge. When we turned the corner and it got quieter, I happened to glance at Lucas and saw that la-la-land expression that always meant she was about to launch into something about Josh.

So I quick turned to Seneca and said the first thing I could think of, which was, "We told you all about our lives. How about *your* life?"

"My life? I don't have a life." She said it in a really bitter way, like she was trying to sound like a grownup again, but when I glanced at her, I could tell she meant it, because she almost had tears in her eyes.

"But you're famous," I said, "and you get to travel to places, and you've been on talk shows on TV—"

Seneca interrupted what I was saying. "That doesn't

mean I have a life. I don't. I have a *schedule*. I never get to do things that are fun, like we just did. Every day when I'm not on the road, and sometimes when I *am* on the road, I do the same things. I get up at seven. Then I work out, then I practice, then I study with Edie, then I practice—" She broke off. "Like that. A schedule. I've been thinking a lot lately about how much I wish I had a more normal life."

I remembered how I'd thought that Seneca would start out telling us about things that made her life sound great, then we'd find out she was just like us. Instead, almost from the beginning she'd let us know that she didn't much like her life. And what she told us made me realize that in a lot of ways she really wasn't like Lucas and me at all.

"No friends?" Lucas asked in a soft voice.

"Only LaToya. We IM sometimes, but I don't get to spend a lot of time on the computer. I see some of the same musicians over and over on the road. They're nice to me, but they're all older than I am. Paul's trying to change all that. I've heard him talking to Mom. He thinks she's put me under too much pressure."

I couldn't help asking, "Do you think she has?"

Seneca shrugged. "She always says you can't make it to the top without sacrifice and discipline."

"So why do you keep on doing it? Is it just because your mom makes you?" Lucas asked.

Seneca was quiet for a minute, and as I glanced at her

I saw her change, right there next to me, from a sad and lonely girl into a tough and famous professional pianist. "I like being at the top."

There didn't seem to be any answer to that. It was okay if that was what she wanted. But I knew I wouldn't give up having a normal life to be the best at something.

"So what's your schedule like today?" Lucas asked.

"Lessons with Edie until six."

"Have you started your school year already?" I asked. Ours didn't start for another two weeks. In Minnesota, the schools don't start until after Labor Day.

"I don't have any school lessons on the days I perform, and I perform a lot during the year, so I only get a couple of weeks of vacation in the summer."

As we crossed the street to our hotel, I said, "You're not performing here until day after tomorrow, right?" She nodded. "Would you like to come to dinner with us and stay overnight in our room? I don't know if it would be okay with your parents and my mom, but if it is, do you want to?"

"I'd love to!" she said, her voice all excited. Then her face fell. "But I doubt my mother will let me."

"Maybe Paul can talk her into it," Lucas said. "I got the impression she does pretty much whatever he wants."

"Yes. She does." She didn't sound completely happy about it.

7

Miss Bumble

Mom was waiting for us in the lobby, working away at her laptop. Of course she said it was okay for Seneca to hang out with us that night. I knew it would be. But what was miraculous was that when we got up to the suite where Seneca was staying, *her* mom and stepdad were okay with it, too. In fact, they seemed almost excited about it.

"Probably planning to have a romantic night together with the kid out of the way," Lucas muttered as she, Mom, and I walked down the hotel corridor after dropping Seneca off for her lessons.

"And what's the matter with that?" Mom asked, pushing the elevator button. "They've only been married six months. I'm all for giving them time for romance. Romance is a good thing. At least, it seemed to be when I had it, if I remember correctly. It's been so long." She put a hand to the side of her face and gazed up at the ceiling, as if trying to think back on what she sometimes called "those thrilling days of yesteryear." Yes, she actually says things like *yesteryear*. Sometimes I wonder about her.

"How about having a romance with Bill?" Lucas asked as the elevator doors opened and we stepped inside. She was talking about a friend of Mom's we'd met earlier that summer while we were in Amsterdam. "I think he likes you. You could get together with him if you wanted to."

"The problem is, I *don't* want to. Not with Bill."

"Too bad Seneca's stepdad is taken," Lucas said. "He's really hot."

"He's good-looking, I must admit. But . . . I'm not sure how I feel about Paul Didier."

The elevator doors opened onto our floor. I said, "You wouldn't like him. Trust me. Remember yesterday afternoon, when we were at that outdoor café and I went into the hotel to get the *Herald Tribune*? I saw him inside, in the coffee shop, and he didn't act like a very nice guy." I told them about seeing Paul with his cell phone, and how mad he was when he couldn't get the number right. "He slammed that phone onto the table—*bam!* I could hear it way out into the lobby. Then he talked to the guy at the desk, who told him what numbers to dial, and he went away without even saying thank you. He stomped out of the hotel. I was surprised there wasn't smoke coming out of his ears."

Mom opened the door to our suite with the key card,

the little white thing that looked like a credit card or library card that fit into the lock on the door. She slept on the fold-out couch so she could have a room to herself, and Lucas and I slept on twin beds in the bedroom.

"You didn't mention any of this to Seneca, did you?"

I shook my head and flopped into a chair. "No, I didn't even have time to tell Lucas until now."

Lucas, who was the last in, closed the door behind her. "We won't say anything to Seneca," she said, before Mom could tell us not to, which she for sure would have done. "The one I don't like is Edie. She is *so fakey!*"

"I don't think Seneca's mom is all that great, for that matter," I added.

Mom tossed her computer case onto the couch. "I'm not saying anything about this. It's not nice to talk about people behind their backs. Besides, I don't want you guys even accidentally quoting me saying something negative about somebody."

Seneca's eyes were shining again when we picked her up for dinner, and she was even more excited when dinner was over and Mom left the three of us alone in our room.

While we cleaned up for bed, it got to be more and more obvious that Seneca was having an awesome time. She loved it when we all crowded into the bathroom together, washing faces and brushing teeth, and every so often I'd see her look at Lucas and me in the mirror, those cute little dimples showing, like she couldn't believe she was with us and doing what she was doing. I wondered if when she was staying with her cousin she'd ever done this kind of thing before—ever gone to a slumber party, ever been a part of a bunch of friends just having a good time.

"It's really cool hanging out with you guys," she said when we were all leaving the bathroom. "Are you going to be here for the whole festival?"

"No, we're staying for your concert on Friday night, then we're leaving the next morning," Lucas answered. "We're going to tour the Scottish Highlands with Celia, a good friend of Kari's mom—well, she's our friend, too— who lives in London. But we'll be back for your Tuesday and Friday concerts next week."

Seneca's eyes made it impossible for her to hide what she was feeling, and it was obvious she was disappointed that we were going away for the weekend.

I felt sorry for her. "I kind of wish we weren't leaving," I said. "I'm not all that crazy about sightseeing with my mother, to be honest about it. It would be more fun to stay here with you."

Lucas added, "Yeah, it would be sweet if the three of us could hang out here. Edinburgh is seriously cool, with all the street performers and everything."

Just then Seneca reached into her bag and pulled out a scruffy stuffed rabbit with floppy ears. When she turned around and saw Lucas and me watching her, she looked a little embarrassed. "This is Miss Bumble," she said. "I take Miss Bumble with me everywhere."

Lucas and I didn't make a big deal about the stuffed animal, but seeing Seneca with her bunny almost made me want to cry. I remembered how I once felt about my teddy bear, Thumb. I'd always thought of him as my best friend, and I wondered if that's how Seneca felt about Miss Bumble. After all, except for her cousin, who else did she have? I decided I really wanted Lucas and me to stay in Edinburgh to show her what it was like to be a normal teenager. She was a nice person. She deserved to have friends who weren't stuffed animals, and a life that was more than a schedule. No matter how much she wanted to be at the top.

8
What the Tarot Cards Told Us

"I have an idea. Before we go to bed, let's do a tarot reading," Lucas said.

That night at dinner Lucas had set what I figured was a new record for *not* talking about Josh Daniels. Maybe the trip was working. Anyway, she'd been Josh-free for about as long as she could manage, and I figured that now she wanted me to pull out the tarot cards we'd brought along so we could read Mr. Makes Me Want to Gag into her future.

I'm not sure I really believe in tarot cards any more than I believe in ghosts, but they can be fun, like reading your horoscope or analyzing handwriting. My dad had bought me a tarot set earlier in the summer. I hadn't gotten very good at reading the cards—they always seemed to say something different, even when I put them down twice in a row for the same person.

Anyway, I got the deck out and we pulled the two beds together, turned out the overhead light, turned on Lucas's Itty Bitty Book Light, and started our reading. The book light was on the bed by the cards, and the little glow shining upward made eerie shadows on the wall and on our faces.

I started out doing a spread for Lucas, and no matter how many times she shuffled and I put the cards down, I couldn't make it look like she was going to find true love. Even *she* couldn't make the cards say that. In fact, they were kind of a mess. The only things that really fit with what was happening in our lives were something about transportation and something about friendship. Otherwise it was all about new things and hard things—like I said, it didn't really make much sense.

When we finished with Lucas, I said, "Okay, Seneca, your turn. What do you want to know?"

"Um, I suppose . . . how things will go for me during Festival."

She shuffled and I set the cards out. Ten cards in the Celtic Cross spread.

The card I put down in the indicator place, which means the main issue, seemed right for what I was doing. It was the Temperance card, which sometimes means art. And the fifth card, which went up on top, was the Queen of Wands, which was an attractive, artistic woman, so that was probably Seneca.

But the rest of the spread gave Seneca a terrible fortune. The Tower card was in the position that stood for what was going to happen next, which seemed to show that Seneca was going to go through something terrible and sudden. The influence over the situation was the King of Cups in reversed position, which was a man who was violent or wicked. The rest of the cards weren't any better. There was a Knight of Wands—the same card that I had thought meant transportation in Lucas's reading, which was the only thing I could remember that card standing for. But there probably were other things it stood for, too, since transportation didn't seem to make sense. The upside-down Seven of Pentacles meant desire for money. And there were two more Seven cards: of Swords and of Wands. All the Seven cards mean struggle, and with three Sevens in the spread, the struggle seemed incredible. The card that showed the final outcome was the High Priestess—which might mean serenity, or might mean intuition, or might just mean that things stayed hidden.

I couldn't believe it could be this bad, so I said, "Uh-oh. I did something wrong. Just a second and we'll start again."

Seneca shuffled, handed me the deck then hugged Miss Bumble to her stomach. She was engrossed in what was going on. Beyond her was Lucas, whose expression showed she knew what the cards had meant and what I was doing.

Because of the way the dark shadows fell on their faces, both of them looked like strangers. I suppose I looked the same way to them. It was almost scary.

And then something *really* spooky happened: the second time I put the cards down, I got a spread almost as bad as the one before, and even with some of the same cards. The Queen of Wands, Seneca's card, moved to the number-one spot. And the influence card was now the reversed Queen of Swords, which meant an unscrupulous woman—sneaky, and maybe a liar. There were only two Seven cards this time, but that still meant plenty of struggle.

And the final outcome? The High Priestess card again. Wow.

My mom has a saying that goes, "This situation calls for diplomacy." It means she has to find a way of dealing with a tricky problem by doing or saying something that doesn't cause trouble or hurt people's feelings. I figured if there was ever a situation that called for diplomacy, this was it.

"Uh-oh, looks like you're going to have a little bit of trouble," I said, only I used the happiest tone of voice I could come up with just then, like the trouble could be as small as breaking a shoelace or getting a fruit juice stain on a favorite hoodie.

I hadn't looked up since dealing the cards the second time. Now I did. Seneca was still leaning over them, this time with a puzzled expression. But Lucas was looking straight at me, with her teeth on her lower lip and a worried expression on her face.

"What does this card mean?" Seneca asked.

"Well," I said, "that's the Queen of Swords, and where it is, above that indicator card there, means she's the influence in the situation. Some tarot readers believe in reversed positions and some don't—"

Before I could come up with any more diplomacy, Seneca interrupted me.

"It looks just like Edie!"

Lucas picked up her book light and held it directly over the Queen of Swords. The woman on the card was looking off to the side and had her chin tilted into the air exactly like Edie always did, plus the shape of her chin and her nose, even the color of her hair, were like Edie's. If Edie wore a long wig, she would have looked almost exactly like that.

"I don't want Edie influencing me!" Seneca said. "I can't stand her."

"Is she really that bad?" Lucas asked. Meanwhile I reached out, ready to scoop the cards up and stick them back in their box.

But Seneca caught my hand. "Please wait, Kari. I want to hear some more." Then, answering Lucas's question, she said, "Edie is just a . . ."

"Meep?" Lucas asked. Then she explained that we used the word *meep* when we wanted to say a bad word but weren't supposed to.

"*Meep*. I like that." Seneca laughed, and her smile was bright in the dark room. "That's a perfect way of describing her."

"Well, it took us about a minute and a half to decide we didn't like her, either," Lucas said.

"It was obvious she was sucking up to Mom," I said.

"She sucks up to everybody. Let's change the subject. I don't want to waste our time talking about her. Tell me the rest of the fortune, Kari."

I'd been thinking while they'd been talking, and now I was ready with what to say next. "Well, the difference between the last fortune and this one is that in the last one some man was the big influence, and now it's a woman," I said, avoiding the bad fortune itself.

"Paul?" Seneca asked.

I shrugged. "I don't know. It doesn't say. Could it be your real father?"

She shook her head. "My real father died in a car accident when I was five."

"Was he a musician, too?" Lucas asked, and I shot her a thankful look for changing the subject.

"Yes, he was a concert pianist," Seneca said. "African American, as you could probably figure out," she added, and her dimples showed again. "He wanted to go onstage and have a career, like I have. Mom says he was a great pianist, but he was almost twenty years older than Mom, and there was more racial discrimination when he was starting out. Mom says he never had a fair chance or he would have been a big star. He taught classical piano, and that's how they met. They both taught piano in the same music conservatory. He also liked playing jazz. That's maybe why I like *Rhapsody in Blue*, which is kind of half jazz, half classical. Anyway, part of the reason Mom pushes me so hard is because of my dad. She's doing it for him."

"How did your mom get together with Paul?" Good old Lucas was making sure Seneca didn't notice as I stacked all the cards and put them in the box.

"We hired him as my manager, and she fell for him right away. He bought her presents and took her to expensive restaurants. He had flowers delivered every single day. And he was unbelievably charming to Mom. He has a reputation in the music world for being charming. I have a feeling he could have had any woman he wanted. Everywhere we go, women want to be around him. You should have seen Edie."

This sounded like good gossip. "Edie likes him?"

"She had a crush on him when Mom and Paul first got married. She seems to have gotten over it."

"What did your mom say about that?" Lucas asked.

"I don't actually think she noticed."

"You've never said how *you* feel about Paul," I said.

Seneca was quiet for a minute. "As I said, Paul's made Mom *and* Edie be . . . more lenient to me, and that's good. But I don't especially—" She broke off from whatever it was she'd started to say, and instead said, "To be honest, sometimes I feel like he's taking Mom away from me."

She looked up, as if changing the subject, and said, "Anyway, what are your dads like?"

I told her about how my dad is a professional artist who lives on a houseboat on the Mississippi River. I talked about how he taught me to paint and draw, and how I stay with him in the summer and he takes me out fly-fishing, and it's always fun for about a week. But by then it gets obvious that he wants me out of the way so he can have his girlfriends over and have parties and drink too much—in fact, a couple of times women had dropped in to visit him on the boat when I was there, although Mom didn't know or she'd never have let me go back.

Lucas told about her dad, a big-deal lawyer who works on international cases, and how we call him Allen the Meep because he's so mean to everybody, except her little brother. Then she told about her mother, Camellia (we call her the Fair Camellia), who's gorgeous, and from the South, and still talks with a big fake southern accent when she's trying to impress somebody, and how Allen and Camellia fight all the time.

Lucas said she thought her mom only stayed with Allen because he makes tons and tons of money. And then she said that he'd been treating her, Lucas that is, better ever since we solved the mystery of the forged Rembrandt painting called *The Third Lucretia*.

Seneca said, "You solved a mystery? That is *so cool.* Was it fun?"

"We liked figuring things out," Lucas said, "and tracking down the guy who did it."

"But it was scary, too," I added. "Lucas almost got run over in London, and later, when we were in Amsterdam, we got into this terrible part of town, and I was afraid I might actually get murdered or something. Then Mom and Lucas got caught. . . ."

We told Seneca all about it. When we were finished, she said, "That's amazing! The two of you must have an incredible amount of courage."

"That's what everybody said afterward," I said. "Lucas is actually brave. I call her Lucas the Lionheart or Nerves of Steel Stickney. But I'm not brave at all. Sometimes I was so scared I was almost sick."

"But you did it anyway," Lucas said. "That's what being brave is: being afraid but doing it anyway. Don't put yourself down, Kari."

"Mostly I'm pretty timid, at least in my regular life," Seneca said. "I wonder if I'd be brave if something happened to me. I'd like to think I would be, since Scottish people are famous for being brave, and I'm part Scottish. I wish I could have an adventure and find out."

Later, when I thought about what Seneca said that night, I remembered the saying, *Be careful what you wish for, because you just might get it.*

9
Planning for the Weekend

The next day, Thursday, Mom and Lucas and I went to hear the whole orchestra rehearse. I was used to seeing musicians at concerts looking all stiff and fancy in black dresses for the women and tuxedos for the men. But this time they wore jeans and casual tops. Even Alexander Cameron, the conductor, was wearing black jeans and a T-shirt.

Seneca couldn't stay over again that night because she needed to get her sleep before the performance, which was on Friday. But Mom and Lucas and I had dinner together with Seneca and her mom, her stepdad, and Edie, who was wearing another black pantsuit. (I wondered if she ever wore anything *but* black pantsuits.) Mom said that for this meal she was going to go "off the clock," as she put it, which meant this would be just for fun—she wouldn't be working, wouldn't be interviewing anyone, and wouldn't be taking notes.

During dinner, Paul was extremely charming to Mom. Even though I'd seen him lose his temper, I could see why people liked him, especially women. In fact, everybody was having a good time. Edie seemed almost excited, somehow, and Seneca's mom asked us to call her Teresa instead of Mrs. Didier.

When we were eating dessert, Paul turned to Mom and said, "Seneca tells us you're leaving for the Scottish Highlands the day after tomorrow."

"Right," Mom answered. "Our friend Celia is driving up from London early Saturday morning. She'll pick us up here, and we'll start toward Inverness in the afternoon."

"Could she come and hear Seneca play tomorrow night?" Paul asked.

"Unfortunately not. Celia's an arts marketing consultant and she has an important presentation to one of her clients, some big theater, on Friday afternoon. She'll be at the Tuesday concert. Maybe Seneca can stay overnight with Kari and Lucas after tomorrow night's performance. Would that be okay?"

"Mom, don't forget, Lucas and I are babysitting after the concert." Laura Weiss had called and asked if we could watch Parker. It was the Weisses' anniversary, and she and her husband wanted to go out to dinner when the performance was over. Reyan Ugas, a woman who was on the orchestra staff, was going to watch him all the way through the part where Seneca played, which was right before intermission. Then Lucas and I were going to take charge of him. That wouldn't be until about nine o'clock, but Laura said that Parker had been taking long naps since they'd gotten to Edinburgh, so it would be okay for him to stay up late.

Lucas turned to Seneca. "Want to babysit with us?"

"I'd love to! I've never ever babysat in my whole life." I could hardly believe it. "May I? Please?" Seneca asked, looking at her mom and stepdad.

For some reason, Paul first looked at Edie instead of at Teresa, and for a minute I thought he was going to say no. Then he turned back to Mom. "This would be in the Weisses' room, I take it?"

She nodded. "The Weisses will give them money to take a taxi from the concert hall to the hotel."

"Well"—he hesitated—"sure. That'll be fine. They can babysit together, then stay overnight in your room. Which brings us to another proposition. Seneca suggested, and Teresa, Edie, and I all agree, that it would be nice if Kari and Lucas could spend the weekend here in Edinburgh with us."

"You mean, stay here while I go up to Inverness?" Mom asked.

"Exactly," Paul said, then turned to us. "What do you think, kids?"

Seneca looked at Lucas and me, her eyes sparkling.

"That would be awesome!" Lucas said.

"Yeah, seriously!" I said, and meant it. This was exactly what I'd been hoping for. I like Celia, but she'd be with us Monday and Tuesday, so we'd have a chance to spend time with her then. And meanwhile, it would be a lot more fun hanging with Lucas and Seneca in Edinburgh than driving around looking at scenery with Mom and Celia, who would probably sit in the front seat and talk about boring stuff the whole time.

"I . . . I don't know," Mom said. "That's a lot of burden for you."

Paul leaned across the table toward Mom and looked right into her eyes. "Being with girls her age has already been good for Seneca. She gets far too nervous before her concerts, especially the important ones. We want her as relaxed as possible. It would be a favor to us."

"Celia has a cell phone," I said to Mom. "If you leave yours with us, we can text and stuff." Mom's cell worked all over the world, but Lucas and I had left ours at home because they didn't work outside the United States.

Mom looked toward Teresa. "How do *you* feel about it?"

Teresa wasn't a very smiley person, but now she gave as much of a smile as she ever really came up with. "I agree with Paul. We'd love to have them."

I wasn't sure she meant it, but it was probably the best we were going to get from her.

10

Scotty MacTarzan, the Casting Queen, and Other Little Things

It had rained off and on the day before, and even on the days when it hadn't rained, it had been cool. Mom said that was typical for Scotland. But Friday, the day of Seneca's first concert, was warm and sunny. In the morning, Seneca had to rehearse with the orchestra. Then she was allowed to have the afternoon off.

Mom needed to work on her article, but Seneca wanted to see Edinburgh Castle and take a walk on the Royal Mile, and Paul said it would be okay if Lucas and I took her. He said doing a little sightseeing would take her mind off the performance and help her relax.

So after a quick lunch we were off, the three of us, starting with the castle, which Lucas and I had visited on Wednesday afternoon, when Seneca was having her lessons with Edie.

Edinburgh Castle isn't pretty—not like a fairy-tale

castle or anything. But it's really interesting. Kings and queens of Scotland lived there for hundreds and hundreds of years.

We took Seneca to our favorite parts of it: the teeny little chapel built almost a thousand years ago, the room that holds the Scottish crown and scepter and sword, the pet cemetery where soldiers who guarded the castle buried their dogs, and the dungeon, which must have been pretty scary back when they kept prisoners there.

I've noticed how often it is that things can seem totally random and normal when they're going on, and it's not until later, when you look back at them, that you realize they were super important to how things turned out. That's how it was with almost everything that happened that afternoon.

We walked all the way down to the Palace of Holyroodhouse at the end of the Royal Mile, then started back up. Along the way we bought a piece of cake at a takeout bakery and wandered around until we found a place to eat: a graveyard behind a little church where we could sit on the grass under a tree. There'd been a cemetery outside every church we'd seen in Edinburgh so far.

We were finishing the cake when Seneca asked us if we did any sports. We told her about the softball team that Lucas and I play on in the summer, and cross-country skiing in the winter, Lucas's gymnastics at school and my tennis lessons, and about the karate we'd been taking with Mom ever since our adventure in Amsterdam.

"Next summer I want to learn how to do rock climbing," Lucas said. "I took a one-day course at REI last spring and I wanted to take the course this summer, but the class was already full."

"Wow, that's a lot of sports!" Seneca said.

"Well, we're not all that great at everything," I said. "Like, Mom is way better than we are in karate, because she took lessons when she was younger."

"But there's something Kari's really good at," Lucas said. "Ask her about her fishing."

"Okay, I'll rise to the bait, ha-ha," Seneca said.

"Very funny," I said, and Lucas groaned. I noticed that the more Seneca was around us, the happier and more like us she seemed.

"What about this fishing?"

I shook my head and rolled my eyes. "It's no big deal." Lucas was chowing down the last bite of cake. I reached for our crumpled-up napkins and shoved them into the paper bag. "My dad and I fly-fish together, and this summer I won the junior casting contest in his little town."

Lucas swallowed and put her used fork in the bag.

"She even got a trophy for it," Lucas said. "She likes to kiss it every night before she goes to bed."

"Shut up, Lucas, or I'll tell how you follow Josh Daniels when he leaves Café Olé just to look at the back of his head."

We both stuck our tongues out at each other at the same time, and all three of us burst out laughing.

When we finally stopped, Seneca said, "This probably sounds like a stupid question, but what's casting?"

"It's when you, like, get the fishing line to go way out in the water by just throwing it with what's called a fly rod." Seneca's face looked blank. "It's a kind of fishing pole you use in a special kind of fishing, called fly-fishing. Are you able to do any sports with your, um, schedule?" I asked. My question was as much to change the subject as anything. I was getting a little tired of Lucas always teasing me about the casting contest.

"Not exactly sports, but I can do this." She got to her feet, jumped up to grab the tree branch above us, and quickly and smoothly swung herself, using one hand after the other, almost all the way to the end of the branch, then turned herself around and started back the way she'd come.

"Wow!" Lucas said. "How did you get so strong?"

Seneca laughed and kept going. "Remember when I said I do an hour of exercises every morning? Well, most of them are for my shoulders and arms and hands. By the way, my mom would kill me if she knew I was doing this without gloves on. Pianists have to worry about their hands, you know."

She was saying all this while she moved back and forth on the branch like it was the easiest thing in the world. She continued, not even out of breath, "Musicians have to keep their muscles in shape because they do the same movements over and over. We can end up in pain if we're not careful. For me it's pounding on the piano. So I do lots of push-ups and pull-ups. I have great shoulder and arm muscles."

Lucas rolled her eyes. "Here I am, hanging out with Scotty MacTarzan and the Junior Casting Queen of Wabasha, Minnesota."

Seneca dropped to the ground, then sat down and hugged one of her knees. "I wish I could do some normal sports like you do. I haven't exactly mentioned this but I'm . . . I've been thinking of making a major change."

"What kind of change?" Lucas asked.

"I'm thinking of, um . . . retiring for a while. From performing, I mean. Not from playing. I love playing, and I want to have a concert career. Just . . . later. Take a few years off to live a normal life."

Lucas and I stared at her for a minute.

"Wow!" I said. "That's a pretty big decision!"

"Is this something you've just decided, or have you been thinking about it for a while?" Lucas asked.

Seneca, still hugging her knee, glanced over at one of the gravestones. "I've been kind of thinking about it for a long time." She looked back at us. "I guess I told you I don't really like my life. My schedule. Being with you guys has made me realize how much I want to be *normal*, for a change. Having a concert career now, when I'm so young, wasn't exactly my idea. Or maybe I should say, I'm not so much doing it for me, I'm more doing it for my mother. And even, in a way, for my father, who's been dead all these years, if that makes any sense."

We both nodded.

"Anyway, like I said, it's not as if I want to give up the piano, so I'll still have to spend hours every day practicing. I *do* like to perform, and I *do* like to be the best. But I want to have some time to live like other kids my age."

"So, when are you going to tell your mom about this?" Lucas asked.

Seneca lowered her knee and picked a blade of grass. "I don't know. Mom is going to want to kill me. It makes me scared just to think about it."

We stood up to go. "I think you should just do it," Lucas said, dusting the grass and dirt off the seat of her pants. "After all, it's your life, and your career."

Such a Lucas thing to say! I wasn't as brave as she was, so I could understand exactly how Seneca felt.

"Just a second while I finish this paragraph." Mom was sitting on the couch and typing away on her computer. A minute later she hit a final key with a big flourish, then moved the computer off her lap.

"So how'd it go with Seneca?"

We told her all about touring the castle and about eating the cake in the graveyard.

"Seems an odd place for a picnic, but evidently tastes differ on these things," Mom said. "Hey, there's been a change in plans. Pack up your suitcases, because you're staying in Seneca's room tonight."

Turns out, Celia had called while Lucas and Seneca and I were hanging out. The big boss at the theater where she was supposed to make her presentation had come down with strep throat, and her meeting had been postponed. She was starting from London and would get to Edinburgh that night. Since it was impossible to find anywhere to spend the night or even park her car in Edinburgh during Festival—surprise, surprise, with two and a half million people in town—she was going to pick up Mom at intermission, right after Seneca finished playing, and drive out of town. They'd look for a room somewhere along the way to Inverness.

"Is this okay with, like, Teresa and Paul?" Lucas asked.

"Well, with, like, Teresa anyway," Mom said. "She said it was, like, fine. Paul had, like, already, like, gone to be at the hall for, like, the piano tuning."

She always does this to me. I made sure not to smile. It only encourages her.

"You mean Teresa gave permission for Seneca to do something fun even without Paul making her do it?" Lucas asked.

"Believe it or not, she did," Mom answered. "I know. I was as surprised as you are. Be prepared, this may signal the end of civilization as we know it."

∾ ∾ ∾

On our way to dinner, we stopped at Seneca's family's suite on the sixth floor. Lucas and I brought our suitcases with our stuff for the weekend, and Mom wanted to leave information on where she could be reached on the road.

Teresa and Seneca were alone at a table by the window in Paul and Teresa's sitting room, finishing a couple of big salads. The room was huge. It must have been sometimes used for meetings and things, because it even had its own bathroom.

Seneca, her parents, and Edie had side-by-side rooms, with connecting doors that led from one to the other on the inside. We wheeled our suitcases into Seneca's room, which was between Paul and Teresa's sitting room on one side and Edie's room on the other, then came back to where Mom was giving Teresa a piece of paper.

"Here's the number for the hotel where we're staying in Inverness," Mom was saying. "It's called . . ."

Mom's voice went on, but I was too busy watching Seneca to listen very closely. Seneca was nervous and jumpy this close to her performance, walking around the room and picking up things and putting them down the whole time our moms were talking. For the concert, we'd brought a pair of opera glasses, which are like little binoculars people take to operas and concerts to be able to see the stage better. I had them around my neck. Seneca asked if I would take them off so she could look through them.

"Let's see if I can spy on somebody." She moved to the window and looked out over the bridge. "Four of the horn players just went into a pub. Alexander Cameron and that pretty blonde from the cello section are heading off together. I wonder if they have something going."

In the background, Mom said something about Celia's cell phone number. "That reminds me, Kari, here's *my* phone," she said, and handed it to me.

"If you need to reach me," she said to Teresa, "you'll have to do it by telephone because I'm hoping not even to touch a computer while I'm away."

I was only half listening. I walked into the other room and put Mom's phone on Seneca's dresser. We couldn't have it turned on in the concert hall anyway, so there was no sense taking it with us.

I heard Seneca say, "Edie's over on Princes Street talking to a guy in a green striped shirt. Must be a cab driver. Two women from the violin section are walking across the bridge looking at a map."

Then it was time for us to go. Seneca had asked us to bring the tarot cards so we could do another reading after Parker went to bed. I wasn't sure that was such a good idea, but we'd brought them anyway. Since Seneca seemed so interested in the cards, I gave them to her to take backstage so she could look at the instruction book while she waited to perform. Then we all wished Seneca luck, Lucas and I said we'd come to her dressing room right after she played, and we gave her big hugs and left for dinner.

Like I said, this all seemed totally random at the time. But if things hadn't happened just like they did—the changes in Mom's travel plans, the cake in the cemetery, the cell phone on the dresser, what Seneca saw through the opera glasses, even the tarot cards—the story would have happened in a very different way.

11

The Concert

After dinner, Mom, Lucas, and I walked to the Usher Hall, entered through the front doors instead of the stage door for a change, and took our seats.

When I first met Seneca, I'd thought of her as a star, and it was hard thinking of her as a real person. Now that we'd gotten to know her, that was completely switched around. Now I thought of her as a person, and had trouble remembering she was a star.

But the concert that night reminded me. I can still see the whole thing as if it was happening this very minute. When we walked in, the Usher Hall was crowded with people. Some of the guys were wearing kilts, and Lucas and I nudged each other. I wondered how a person could find out if it was true about them not wearing underwear, but except for crawling around on the floor, I couldn't think of a way. At last we sat down in the hall, which now seemed so familiar to us.

We watched for ten minutes or so while the musicians trickled into their seats onstage—the women wearing long black dresses and high heels, the men in tuxedos with tails worn over white shirts and white bow ties. I knew from rehearsal that we were going to have to get through one whole piece before it was time for Seneca to play.

A couple of times over the past two days I'd thought about Seneca's terrible tarot reading. Like I say, I didn't really take the tarot thing seriously. Still, it was enough to make me worry that the concert was going to be some kind of total disaster. When I thought about that, my chest got tight with nervousness, and it was hard to take a deep breath.

Finally the lights went dim, the orchestra tuned up, the audience got quiet, and Alexander Cameron came out. Everybody clapped, and the first piece started.

Because it was an American orchestra, they were playing all American music. This piece was called *Adagio for Strings* by a guy named Barber. I'd liked it when I heard the orchestra rehearsing, but to be honest, I was so nervous for Seneca that I just wanted it to be over. When they were done playing there was this long time while the audience applauded. Then a couple of guys came onstage and rearranged everything. Like you can tell from its name, *Adagio for Strings* was played just by the string instruments, but the orchestra for *Rhapsody in Blue* was a lot bigger. So a bunch more musicians came out and sat down, including

Parker's parents, and the whole tuning-up business started again.

At last everybody was ready and it was quiet in the concert hall. Seconds passed; it seemed like hours. Finally the side door opened, and out came Seneca in a long, elegant lavender dress, with Alexander Cameron behind her.

She looked amazing! She walked to the piano, bowed while the audience clapped, sat down, and moved the piano bench back and forth. When she got it in just the right place, she looked up at Alexander Cameron and nodded her head for him to begin.

I got over being nervous after about the first five notes. I've been going to concerts with Mom since I was little, and one thing I've noticed is that sometimes they're more exciting than others, not because of the music, but just because of, like, a mood or energy in the audience that makes the orchestra play better. Mom calls it "electricity in the hall." There must have been a lot of electricity in the hall that night because *Rhapsody in Blue* sounded even more wonderful than it had in rehearsal.

It was awesome, and Seneca was the star of it all. I couldn't take my eyes off her. She was totally focused. Sometimes she was playing slowly and softly, sometimes she was bending way to her right and using both hands to play something tinkly on the very highest keys. In some of the jazzy parts she moved her shoulders with the rhythm, and in the most exciting parts she pounded the piano so hard the muscles showed in her arms. The music and her playing were so incredibly good that it gave me goose bumps.

The minute it was over, the audience members jumped to their feet. Seneca stood up, her face all sparkling eyes and dimples. Alexander Cameron kissed her on both cheeks, the orchestra stood up, and Seneca turned to shake hands with the concertmistress, which is another name for the first violinist. Seneca and Alexander went backstage, then came out and took another bow.

After two more curtain calls, Seneca sat back down at the piano and played her encore, the Chopin piece. It was so beautiful that Mom ended up with tears in her eyes.

When the piece was over and the clapping started, Mom signaled to us with her head, and the three of us left the auditorium.

We walked outside to the curb, where Celia was waiting in her car. Celia's cool. She's blond and slim and pretty, with great clothes and fashionable glasses and haircut. We'd gotten to know her and her friend Robert when we were in London. We like her especially because she knows how to talk to kids, which is more than most adults do.

It was good to see her if only for a minute, and fun to know we'd be hanging out in Edinburgh with her when she and Mom got back from the Highlands. We said good-bye, and the car drove off.

∾ ∾ ∾

Instead of going back into the lobby, which we knew would be a sea of people now that it was intermission, we went around the building to the stage entrance. My heart was still pumping from the excitement of the concert, and I couldn't wait to tell Seneca what a great job she'd done.

Right inside the stage entrance was a door that said ARTISTES' SUITE, which led to the dressing rooms for the guest artists. We went through into the little entry area, and Lucas knocked at Seneca's room.

No answer.

She knocked again, and yelled, "Seneca, it's us."

Nothing.

Paul, Teresa, and Edie, who'd also been sitting in the audience that night, came through the artists' door into the entry. Paul said something, and Edie, striding along in a black pantsuit and stiletto heels as usual, let out one of her too-loud laughs. Everyone seemed high with excitement. Teresa smiled at us and opened Seneca's door, leading the way into the empty dressing room. "She's probably in the bathroom," she said.

We stood around for a minute waiting for Seneca, laughing and talking about how well she'd played, how the audience had cheered, how many bows she'd taken, what the critics would say. The minute got longer.

I turned to Lucas and whispered, "I'd better go get Parker."

I went back out through the artistes' suite door and

down a hall crammed with instrument cases, to a room with a sign that said GREEN ROOM. It was full of even more instrument cases, and huge square crates on wheels, some for instruments and some that held the gowns and tuxedos for the traveling musicians. Orchestra members and other people, most of them dressed in black, were coming and going everywhere. Parker was there with Reyan.

"Here he is." She looked relieved to see me. "Keep an eye on him. He likes to escape. He got away from me twice tonight. And once he pulled off my scarf!" she said with a smile. When Laura had introduced us to her, Reyan had said she was Somali. Like most Somali women—we have a lot of them in Minnesota—she was Muslim and wore a head scarf.

"Be a good boy, Parker," she said, and gave him a big hug.

"We'll take good care of him," I said, and took his hand, and the two of us walked back out of the greenroom, down the hall, and into the artists' area.

For as long as I live, I'll never forget what I saw when I got to Seneca's open doorway. The room, which had been so full of excitement when I'd left it, was now absolutely quiet. Everyone inside was standing as if they were frozen. The only movement came from the TV screen, which showed the Usher Hall stage where some guy was walking around rearranging the chairs the orchestra members sat in.

The door that led to the bathroom was open—obviously Seneca wasn't there. Lucas was on one side of the room, scrunched next to a tall, fancy clock like she was trying to be invisible. Teresa leaned on a baby grand piano in the corner, her back toward me. Edie had an arm around her. Both women stared at Paul, who stood by the piano bench. He had a piece of paper in his hand.

The scene stayed like that for maybe seven seconds. Then, with a jerk, Teresa pulled away from Edie, stepped to where Paul was standing, and snatched the paper from him. She glanced down at it for a minute, turned around, and looked straight at Parker and me. Her eyes were full of tears and terror.

For a second her mouth moved as if she was trying to say something but couldn't get the words out.

"They've . . ." she started, still looking toward Parker and me. "Somebody's . . ." Her voice trailed off and she turned to Paul.

He put his arms around her, then looked over her head at me. "Seneca's been kidnapped," he said.

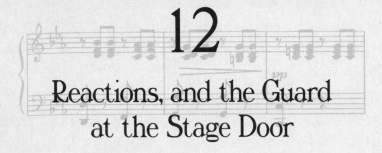

12

Reactions, and the Guard at the Stage Door

I kept standing in the doorway, not because I was too shocked to move but because I actually couldn't walk. Parker must have sensed the terror in the room around him, and he was holding on to my legs for dear life, his face buried in my skirt.

Teresa grabbed at Paul's lapels with both her hands. "But what are we going to *do*? We've got to *do something*!" Her voice sounded frantic, almost hysterical, and tears were streaming down her cheeks.

Paul pulled her close again and held her tight against him, rubbing her back and trying to calm her. "She'll be safe, darling," he said, his cheek lying on top of her head. "They say as long as we don't go to the police, they won't hurt her. All they want is the money. They won't hurt her if we give them the money." For a minute they stood there while Teresa sobbed quietly.

"What exactly does the note say?" Edie asked, her voice sounding loud and intense in the quiet.

Teresa moved out of Paul's arms. Her face was shiny with tears and streaked with mascara, and there were black mascara marks on Paul's shirt. She handed the note to Edie.

"'We have your daughter,'" Edie read. "'She will be safe if you pay us five hundred thousand pounds. You must tell no one. If the police learn of this, Seneca will be killed. We will contact you.'"

By this time I'd dragged Parker into the room. He tried to make a run for it, but I got hold of his arm, then his hand, and held it in an iron grip.

Parker's squirming got Paul's attention. He frowned. "Why's this kid here?"

Lucas stepped away from the clock and looked him in the eye. "We're babysitting him. Remember?"

"But he's not supposed to be *here*!"

"Why not? Where else would he be?" Like I said, Lucas doesn't take meep from anybody.

Paul hesitated a second as if trying to find an answer to Lucas's question, and instead turned to me. "Where's your mother?"

"She's, um . . ." I hesitated. Obviously no one had told Paul about the new plan. "She and our friend from London are driving out of town tonight."

"*What*?" Paul exploded. He was obviously extremely

meeped. The tone of his voice rang a bell somehow, but before I could figure out what I was reminded of, Edie broke in.

"She wasn't supposed to leave until morning!"

Teresa was crying again, her face red and twisted, but she took some gasping breaths to stop sobbing and said, "Gillian talked to me about leaving town tonight. It was right after you and Edie left for the piano tuning." She held back another sob. "There was no way of knowing . . ." She trailed off, and looked at us with a face that was so full of fear and sadness that I got tears in my own eyes.

"Please, you mustn't tell anyone," she begged. "Please, please, please."

"Of course we won't," Lucas said, her voice solid as a rock.

Then Paul laughed, but it was the way you'd laugh if what you meant was *I can't believe we have these kids around at a time like this.*

I've never felt so completely in the way. Not even when one of my dad's girlfriends stops in to see him when I'm there.

"We won't be any trouble," I said. "Honest. Just forget about us. We'll—"

"You deal with the kids, Edie," Paul said. A look passed between them that was probably his way of telling her he didn't want to be bothered with us. Then, turning in our direction, he added, "And you keep your mouths shut."

From the expression Lucas shot him, I could tell she was seriously meeped off.

Parker pulled on my skirt and said in a soft voice, "What's wrong?"

I'd honestly forgotten about him for a minute there. Now I could see how upset the atmosphere in the room had made him. He looked ready to cry, and that was the last thing anybody needed.

"It's okay, Parker," I said, lifting him up and cuddling him. "We're going to go back to the hotel, and your mommy and daddy will be there in a little while." Then I turned to Lucas and whispered, "Can you grab those cards?" and tipped my head toward the side of the room.

I looked over to where the tarot cards, instruction book, and the box they came in were scattered over the dressing table. Lucas, her face so angry it was white, walked past Paul and Teresa and used her arm to sweep everything together, stuffed it all into the two pockets of her skirt, then turned and stomped to the door with me behind her.

Paul looked at Parker, then back up at us and said, very quietly, but in a tone that was almost threatening, "You'd better figure out a way to keep that kid quiet."

Edie followed us into the little entryway, closing the door behind us.

"Stop here," she said through tight lips before we went out into the backstage hall.

She was obviously worried—who wouldn't be?—but

somehow I had the feeling she was mad at us, and I couldn't figure out why. Finally she turned and said, "As Paul said, you two had better keep your mouths shut until your mother gets back here."

After the treatment we'd gotten from Paul in the dressing room, Edie's remark was just too much. Lucas was mad. And when she gets mad, whoever she's mad at had better look out.

"Look," she said, her teeth clenched, "this is a terrible time for everyone. We understand that. But let's get something straight here. Kari and I didn't ask for this to happen. *We* didn't kidnap her, and we're as upset as anyone. Just because something awful has happened doesn't give you or Paul or anybody else the right to treat us like garbage. Oh, and by the way, we know perfectly well how to 'keep our mouths shut,' as you and Paul put it so rudely."

Edie looked at Lucas, startled. She was silent for a couple of seconds. Then she sniffed, finally managed her suck-up smile, and said, "I'm sorry. It's just—"

Lucas, who had now taken charge, at least in her own mind, interrupted. "Fine. Kari and I don't need any help from you. We're going back to the hotel and we'll be staying in Kari's mother's room. Don't worry, it's reserved straight through until next week. That's room three fourteen, for your information. For the next few hours, if you need us you can call the Weisses' room. We'll be there babysitting Parker. One more thing . . ."

Edie was following her every word with a sick, fake smile on her face.

"Parker's parents expect Seneca to be with us. What story do you want us to tell them? And what do we tell Kari's mom?"

Edie hesitated for only a second. "You'll have to tell Laura and Earl Weiss that Seneca has a bad sore throat. As for Gillian, you'd better leave it to Paul to contact her. She's a friend, but she's also a member of the press." She shook her head, as if to clear her brain. "I don't know what we're going to do."

I was pretty sure Edie wasn't finished, but that didn't stop Lucas from opening the door to the backstage hall. Edie followed us out from the artists' entryway. Two steps later and there we were, looking right at the stage door, and there was nobody there. I'd been too excited to pay attention when we'd come in, but now I realized the guard hadn't been on duty then either. Which was odd. Normally you had to sign in and out. It made sense that there should have been a guard on pretty much all the time, and especially during a performance, to make sure nobody got in who didn't belong there.

With all the tension going on between them, Lucas and Edie hadn't noticed. But to me it was obvious that something was wrong. Even if the guard had stepped out to go to the restroom, he should have been back by now.

Parker, who'd absolutely wrapped himself around me

the minute Lucas and Edie started in on each other, was getting heavier by the second. Now I put him down in the hall. "Stay here, Parker," I said quietly, and opened the door to the office right next to the entrance.

And for the second time that night I was in for a shock. The guard was lying on the floor.

I didn't want to scare Parker, so I didn't yell, but my heart was pumping so hard I could hear it in my head, and I felt like I couldn't breathe. I walked in, leaned over, and touched the guy's hand. He was warm.

Just then Parker peeked around the corner. "Why's that man sleeping on the floor?" he asked.

"I don't know," I said. I leaned down and put my cheek in front of the man's nose, like I'd seen on TV.

Edie appeared in the doorway, looking from me to the man on the floor. "He's breathing," I said, straightening up. I was trying to be calm for Parker, but I thought my voice sounded panicked. "We've got to call an ambulance. How do you call an ambulance in Edinburgh?"

"I'll do it," Edie said. "Now the three of you go back to the hotel." She crossed the room and reached for the phone on a nearby desk.

We watched her turn toward a list of phone numbers pasted on the wall, and left when she started punching buttons.

As we walked back outside through the stage door, we heard the far-off sound of music. The intermission was over. The second half of the concert had started.

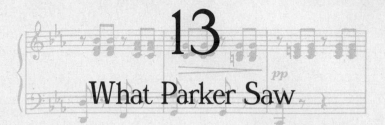

13
What Parker Saw

When we left the building, we just started walking instead of getting a cab. I kept thinking of things I wanted to say to Lucas, but I didn't want to talk about them in front of Parker. He'd already been through a lot that night, and I didn't want him hearing about guards who were hit over the head to get them out of the way so that somebody he knew and liked, the Big Girl Who Played the Piano, could be kidnapped. Lucas was carrying Parker on her shoulders, and now I caught her eye and shot a glance above her head at him. She nodded, and we kept walking without saying a word.

That left me time to think, and there was nothing good to think about. It felt like there was a huge, heavy rock at the bottom of my stomach. I kept wanting Seneca's kidnapping not to be true. I wanted to be able to wake up and have it be over, or know it had never really happened.

It was two very long blocks to the corner, and I'd walked

almost that whole way before I started feeling something even worse: absolute terror for what Seneca must be going through. I wished I could be with her wherever she was, sharing her fear, cheering her up, telling her everything would be all right, helping her find a way out. My stomach clutched up until I felt almost sick, and before I could help myself, tears were coming into my eyes.

I tried to get control of myself for Parker's sake, but I couldn't hold back any longer. I started to cry. Then I felt Lucas's hand on my arm, and I realized she was crying, too. I put my arms around her, including Parker's little legs, and for a minute Lucas and I just stood together crying right there on the sidewalk on Lothian Road in the middle of Edinburgh, with people walking around us on both sides.

"What's wrong, you guys?" Parker said in a very small, trembly voice.

I opened my eyes, and there he was, two inches away, leaning down from his perch on Lucas's shoulders, looking big-eyed right into my face.

I sniffed, and thought about what to say to Parker. At last I said, "We're sad because Seneca's gone and we don't know who she went away with."

"I do," he said.

It was a second before I believed my own ears. Then I gasped, "You *do*?"

"Wait a minute," Lucas said. We were almost to the big

church at the corner. Right beside us, sloping down from an entrance through a stone wall, was another cemetery. The part nearest to us was lit up from the streetlights.

Lucas headed away from the crowded sidewalk and right down into it, and hoisted Parker onto a gravestone so his face was even with ours. Holding on tight so he wouldn't fall, she stood there looking at him. "Now Parker, tell us what you mean. Who did Seneca go with?"

"Some guys."

"What guys?"

"Some mean guys. They talked funny. One guy talked *really* funny, and the other guy talked like Alexander."

The only Alexander I knew was Alexander Cameron, the conductor. Lucas and I looked at each other, and both of us said, "Scottish," at the same time.

"Had you ever seen these guys before?" I asked.

Parker shook his head slowly with a solemn expression, as if this was something he knew for sure. "Can I get down from here? It hurts my bottom," he said. The arch on the top of the gravestone came to a gentle point.

I picked him up and set him back down on a flat gravestone that stuck up less than a foot out of the ground, and Lucas and I got on our knees in front of him.

"What did these guys look like?" Lucas asked.

"One looked like the baker."

"The *baker*?" I exclaimed. "*What* baker?"

"You know. In the neighborhood book."

"What neighborhood book?" Lucas asked.

"*My* neighborhood book!" Parker said, obviously annoyed with us for not knowing what book. "He had a stus-mash."

Lucas and I looked at each other, baffled.

"A *big* stus-mash," Parker said. In the dim light I saw him put his finger crosswise under his nose.

"Mustache!" Again, Lucas and I said the word at the same time.

"What color hair did he have?" Lucas asked.

"Black, silly. Like the baker—"

"In your neighborhood book," I finished for him. "How about the other guy?"

Parker thought about that for a while. "He wasn't very hairy," he answered at last.

I sighed. This could be a long night.

"Do you mean he didn't have much hair?" Lucas asked.

Parker nodded, his head moving way up and way down.

"How much hair did he have?"

I could tell she was trying very hard to keep her voice level.

Parker squeezed his eyes shut. For a minute I thought he was clamming up because he could tell we were impatient, but it turned out he was just thinking. At last the dark brown eyes opened in his incredibly cute little Asian face, and he said, "Like when Daddy doesn't shave."

"I'm talking about the hair on his head," Lucas said.

Parker gave a big nod, as if that was what he was thinking, too.

"Do you mean the hair on his head was really, really, really, really short?" I asked.

Another big nod.

I looked at Lucas. We seemed to be getting somewhere. "Is there anything else you can remember about them, Parker?" I asked.

"They were wearing black clothes, except one guy had green socks."

"Which one had green socks?" Lucas prompted.

"The guy with the really, really, really, really short hair."

"How tall were they?" Lucas asked.

"As tall as men."

Great.

"When did all this happen?" I asked.

"When I hided from Reyan. She got mad at me when I pulled her scarf off, and when she was putting it back on, I ran away and hided."

"Where was Seneca?" I asked. "What did the men say?"

"Can we go someplace where it's light?"

"Sure we can, Parker." Lucas was trying to be soothing. This time she lifted him up onto *my* shoulders. We walked out of the cemetery and to the street corner, then across Princes Street through the crowds to the McDonald's where we'd eaten with Seneca. When we were inside, Lucas took Parker in her lap. I went to the counter and came back with Cokes for us and orange juice for Parker.

It took a while, but we finally managed to squeeze the story out of him. Parker had left the greenroom, heading for the stage door entrance to look outside. On the way he heard someone coming. He thought it was Reyan, and he knew she'd be mad at him, so he hid inside a harp case.

Peeking out of the case, he saw that instead of Reyan, it was the guy with the mustache and the guy with green socks. They'd tied something around Seneca's mouth—Parker called it a "mouth bandage"—and were dragging her out the artistes' suite door. She was wearing a hoodie over her concert dress. When they got to the hall, they picked her up and stuffed her into what Parker called "one of those big instrument boxes."

It was one of the giant wooden crates I'd seen in the greenroom and the hall. "The ones with wheels?" I asked.

His head moved up and down again in that slow nod. "That's for when lots of violins go on trips together." I wondered how many kids his age even knew what the words *instrument* and *harp* meant, and how many knew about traveling crates for violins.

"Then what?" Lucas asked.

Parker, who'd been drinking his orange juice the whole

time, took a couple more sips through his straw. Finally he answered, "Then Seneca saw me, and she got really big eyes."

"You mean she saw you when she was being stuffed in the crate?"

He nodded.

"Then what?" My voice was probably sounding hysterical.

"When the mean guys weren't looking, she did like this in front of her mouth bandage." He put his finger up in a silent *sh* gesture. "And she dropped this on the floor."

Parker reached into the front pocket of his red hoodie, pulled out a tarot card, and held it in both his hands. The big card looked huge compared to his little fists.

"Was she just holding it or did she have it in her pocket, or what?" Lucas asked.

"She was holding it behind her bunny."

So she had taken Miss Bumble.

"What happened then?"

"I stayed hided until they put the box with Seneca in it in their van, and then the van went away. I was scared of the mean guys."

Parker still had the tarot card in his little hands, its back toward me.

Lucas said quietly, "Seneca left a clue." She took the card from Parker and laid it down on the table between us.

It was the Queen of Swords.

14

The Dollhouse Castle in the Sky

"Was this the only card Seneca dropped?" Lucas asked.

Parker nodded again.

Lucas and I looked at each other. I knew we were both thinking about that horrible tarot reading, when Seneca had said the Queen of Swords card looked like Edie. What might have made her think Edie had anything to do with the kidnapping? I couldn't imagine the kidnappers would have talked about it, but I had to ask anyway.

"Parker," I said, "you told us the two guys talked funny. What did they say?"

He obviously loved the slurping sound his straw made when he sucked on it, because he wouldn't answer until he'd sucked up the very last drop of his juice. Finally he said, "They said they were going to take Seneca to the dollhouse castle in the sky."

"What?" I burst out.

"They said they were going to take Seneca to the doll-house castle in the sky," he repeated, exactly like he'd said it before.

"Yes, I heard you, but—"

"The dollhouse castle in the sky?" Lucas asked.

If anything, Parker's nod this time was even bigger and slower than usual. "That's what they said."

"Are you sure that's *exactly* what it was?"

He squeezed his eyes shut, just like he'd done when we were in the cemetery. Finally he opened them and said, "Maybe it was a *little* dollhouse."

"You're sure it was a dollhouse?" Lucas asked.

"In the sky," he answered, his head still going up and down like a pump. "Can we go back and read a book now?"

"We have to talk to your mom about this," Lucas muttered into my ear while we got into a taxi outside the McDonald's. "Do you have the phone number for Celia?"

"Are you kidding?"

"Celia's number will be on your mom's cell phone. You can call her while I'm getting Parker ready for bed."

"Um . . . I don't have Mom's phone."

Now Lucas was the one to say, "What?!"

"I left it on Seneca's dresser."

"You did *what?*"

"Put it on Seneca's dresser! We couldn't have it on

while we were at the concert hall, so I left it there."

"Didn't you think we might need it tonight?"

"Why would I think that?"

"What if Celia had tried to call us during dinner to say she was running late?"

I had to admit, this was something that hadn't occurred to me.

"As soon as Paul and Teresa get back to the hotel, we'll have to call and ask them to give us our phone back," I said.

"Are you serious? As if Paul wouldn't know we were going to call your mother on it! Think of how he treated us in Seneca's dressing room. How do you think asking for our phone would go over?"

"He doesn't have any way of knowing that we don't have Celia's number."

"If we ask for the phone right away, he's sure to figure it out. We do have a phone in our room if we need anything. I think if we ask for the phone tonight, it's going to be a dead giveaway. We at least have to wait until tomorrow sometime before we ask for it back."

"Meep!" It was all I could think of to say.

Parker had had enough of this conversation. He was in my lap, and now he poked me hard in the stomach with his elbow. "What are you guys arguing about?"

"We're just talking about calling Kari's mother," Lucas said.

"Can I talk to her?" Parker said. "I talk to my grandpa and grandma on the phone."

Just then we pulled up at the hotel. As we got out of the car, Lucas muttered, "Do you know the name of the place where they're staying in Inverness?"

"I don't remember. I wasn't really listening."

"I suppose your mom took the computer, too."

"Probably."

"You take Parker up to the Weisses' room. I'll stop at our room on the way up and check. If it's there, maybe we could find the phone numbers and hotels somewhere in her files."

"If it's not just sitting on the desk, she might have locked it in the safe." There was a built-in safe in the closet, where you could put valuable things when you left your room.

"The usual password?"

"I suppose." Mom's "usual password" is 1066, which Mom says is the date of a really famous battle in English history. She uses it as the password for everything.

Lucas got out on the third floor. I got Parker up to the next floor and opened the door to his family's room, but it was hard to concentrate on him instead of on what had happened to Seneca.

I took off his hoodie and hung it in the closet. It wasn't until Parker thumped me on the leg that I realized I hadn't said anything since we got to the room.

"I want to read," he said. He was holding a book called *My Neighborhood Book.* I should have known.

I got on my knees beside him.

"Show me the baker," I said.

He turned the pages with his little hands until we got to the picture of the baker, who was a tall guy with a big dark mustache. "Does the baker really look like one of those guys who took Seneca?" I asked.

Parker gave me that solemn nod again. Then he said, "I'm supposed to sit on your lap while you read to me."

"We'll read. But first we have to get your jammies on," I said.

As I got him ready for bed, the words *key witness* kept coming back to me. Parker was probably the only witness to Seneca's kidnapping, the only person besides Seneca herself who could identify the men who had taken her. Might he be in danger if the kidnappers found out what he knew? And Seneca. My mind flashed back to the note. It was easy enough for Lucas to say that she and I would keep our mouths shut. Parker was another story. What would happen to Seneca if he started telling people what he'd seen?

Parker was all ready for bed when Lucas walked in. To keep him busy, I opened the bottom drawer of the dresser, where his mom had said she kept his toys. I pulled out the five trucks, and in approximately three quarters of a second he was on the floor going, "Vroom vroom."

"No luck," Lucas said, and closed the door behind her. "She couldn't have put it in the safe anyway. It was way too small for a computer. I went down to the front desk to see if she left it in the hotel's safe, but she didn't. She must have taken it."

"Now what?"

Lucas sighed. "Maybe we can e-mail her. The hotel has computers we can use."

"Like I said, I wasn't listening very closely when she was talking to Teresa, but I kind of think she said not to try to get hold of her by e-mail because she wasn't going to be checking it."

"Meep!"

I had a stab of guilt for leaving the phone in Seneca's room. I didn't want Lucas to start in on me for that all over again, so I said, "Want to see the baker?"

I grabbed Parker's book, flipped to the right page, and pointed to the guy with the mustache.

"That's my neighborhood book," Parker said from below us on the floor. "Can we read now?"

"I'm sorry, Parker. Just one more second, I promise." I pulled Lucas over to a corner of the room and whispered, "I think we have to tell Parker not to talk about what he saw tonight."

She looked at me and bit her lip, then whispered back, "I've heard it's not good to ask kids to keep secrets."

"I know. But what could happen if he *did* tell might

be worse than anything that would happen if he *didn't*."

"Maybe we should tell his parents."

"I thought of that. But what if his parents got worried about Parker being a witness and decided to report it to the police, and the kidnappers found out? They said they'd hurt her if anybody went to the police."

She looked down at Parker, then back up at me.

"Yeah, I guess. It's hard to know what's the right thing. Don't you think he'd tell his parents anyway?"

"I have an idea I want to try. We'll see if it works." I took Parker in my lap and asked him if he'd play a game with Lucas and me. The game was that only kids could know about what had happened to Seneca. He couldn't tell any grownups, not even his parents.

"Do you want to play?" I finished, trying to smile and make my eyes sparkle.

"Yeah," he said. "Do I get a prize or something?"

"You get an ice cream cone when we leave Edinburgh if you don't tell any grownups."

He clapped his little hands together. "Can I have chocolate? That's my favorite."

"You can have a chocolate ice cream cone."

"Okay. I won't tell." He snuggled back in my lap. "Now can we read?"

I wondered how good he'd be at keeping the secret. I glanced up at Lucas, who had her hand at her mouth. She looked like she was wondering the same thing.

I took a big breath and started reading *My Neighborhood Book*. When we finished, he wanted to hear it again. By the time we got halfway through the second time, he was asleep.

While we were reading, I noticed Lucas rummaging in her pockets, straightening up the mess of tarot cards that she'd swept off Seneca's dressing table at the theater. She finished just as I got Parker tucked into bed.

I sat back down in the chair I'd been in, and she got up from the floor and sat on the edge of the other one. "That Queen of Swords card Seneca dropped must mean that Edie had something to do with the kidnapping!" She was trying to keep her voice down, but she was so excited that her whisper sounded absolutely fierce.

"That's what I thought, but the trouble is, Edie was in the audience with Paul and Teresa."

"I'm not saying she was the guy with the mustache! I'm saying that somehow Seneca knew that Edie was behind it."

"Yeah, I thought of that. But how? Here Seneca is. She's just finished playing. She and Alexander are out onstage, taking their bows in front of the orchestra. Everybody's clapping. She goes back to her dressing room . . . "

". . . and somebody's waiting for her," Lucas finished for me.

"Okay, so how does Seneca know that Edie's behind it? Does Mustache say to Green Socks, 'Okay, on the count of three, pick the lassie up and dump her in the box, like Edie told us to'?"

"This is no time for jokes," Lucas said.

"But how does Seneca know Edie was part of it?"

"I don't know. But it's something we need to find out if we're going to rescue her."

"Rescue her? *Us*?" This was the real Lucas, thinking we should get right in the middle of this whole kidnapping thing.

"Yes, us! Not maybe rescue her *exactly*, but at least we'll have to be part of it!" She leaned forward in her chair again and used that fierce whisper. "Nobody else knows what we know about this. Except for Parker, and even he doesn't know the connection between the card and Edie."

She pushed her butt back in her chair, but she was still leaning forward. "Don't you see? We can't go to the police!"

"Are you sure? I mean, I know what I just said about Parker and his parents telling the police, and how the kidnappers might hurt Seneca if they found out, but what if we went to them and told them what the note said? That's what the cop shows say you're supposed to do."

"So the police would call Paul and Teresa to see if we were telling the truth, and since the kidnappers told them not to go to the police, they'd probably lie and say she *hadn't* been kidnapped. Do you think they'd listen to a couple of kids instead of Seneca's mother and stepfather?"

I took a big breath. That was one of the problems about being fourteen. It had been a problem in Amsterdam, and now here we were in Edinburgh facing the same thing.

"And we can't risk telling Paul and Teresa what Parker saw," Lucas continued. "They'd never believe what the tarot card meant. Edie would find out. If she was involved in it, she'd probably tell the kidnappers, and then both Seneca *and* Parker could be in danger. It's going to be up to us, Kari."

I thought about this for a while, but I couldn't see any other way out of it. She was right. It *was* going to be up to us. We didn't have any choice. I suddenly remembered wishing for another adventure. What a stupid idea *that* had been!

I heaved a big sigh. "Okay, let's just say the kidnapping was Edie's idea, or at least partly Edie's idea. What do we do next?"

"We get hold of your mom. Right away."

"I can't believe you're so interested in talking to my mother. You're the one who always says, 'Let's not tell your mom about this, we can do it ourselves.' For you to actually want to have her in on this is . . . un-Lucaslike."

She looked down and started picking at the edging of the upholstery. "I know," she said.

"Well, you don't have to be embarrassed about it. I think we should call Mom, too. I'm just wondering why *you* think so."

When she looked back up at me, her expression was way more serious than usual.

"I was thinking while you were taking care of Parker. This is a huge deal, Kari. If we tried something and it went wrong, imagine what might happen to Seneca! Not to mention Parker."

I thought about Seneca, maybe still being driven around in the wooden crate, and I glanced over to Parker asleep on the bed, so adorable and helpless just lying there. I didn't want to think about what could happen to them.

"And here we are in Edinburgh," she continued, "in Scotland for meep's sake, and we don't know anybody or anything. Like, *dollhouse castle in the sky*. Maybe somebody from around here would know what that means. We don't."

You can say that again, I thought. "I'm really sorry I left Mom's phone in Seneca's room. We need it, and we need it now."

"Well, we may be in luck. Guess what was on Seneca's dressing table in the middle of the tarot cards?" She reached into the pocket of her skirt and held up something flat and white: a key card. "No problem getting into Seneca's room," she said.

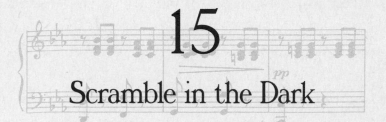

15

Scramble in the Dark

At twelve thirty the Weisses came back, acting very romantic. Laura asked how things had gone with Parker, but she was so busy throwing gaga glances at her husband that she didn't seem to pay attention when I said something about him pulling Reyan's scarf off, and she didn't even ask about Seneca.

We were obviously in the way, so I didn't take the time to give Parker a good-night kiss. But I did give him a glance. Seeing him lying there sleeping and looking so innocent and cute, I got nervous all over again thinking about what might happen to him if anybody knew what he'd seen. When I looked up, Lucas's eyes met mine. She was worried, too.

While we'd waited for the Weisses to get back, we'd come up with a plan to get the phone I'd left on Seneca's dresser. We were going to go to our room and wait until one o'clock, when we thought Teresa, Paul, and Edie would be in bed at least trying to get some sleep. Then we'd sneak up to Seneca's room and use her key card to get in. We thought this was a terrific idea, because if we got caught, we could say we'd come back to get our suitcases. We *would* get our suitcases, for that matter, which would make it not just an excuse, but an actual *reason*.

Trouble was, when we got back to our room, our suitcases were sitting side by side right inside the door. Paul or Edie must have gotten a bellhop or somebody to move them.

"So much for the alibi," I said.

"And I don't suppose they brought the phone," Lucas said.

We looked around for it everywhere we could think of in the room, and when we didn't find it we unpacked absolutely everything in our suitcases, looked in every compartment, even inside the shoes. They hadn't returned the phone.

I flopped down on the couch and blew out a big breath. "Do you think we really have to go up to Seneca's room? I'm totally beat. What if the phone isn't there anymore?"

Lucas flopped next to me. "I know what you mean. If one of them went into the room to get the suitcases instead of just having some staff member do it, they probably saw the phone and took it into the other room or something. But I think we at least have to check."

We sat there for a whole minute, maybe more, not saying a single thing. What with looking through the suitcases, it was way past one o'clock.

Finally I said in a tired voice, "We need a new story."

We decided to say that we'd gone up directly from the Weisses' room to get our suitcases, so we had no way of knowing they'd been moved back to our room. It wasn't a bad alibi. But somehow, even after we came up with it, we didn't move. My eyes wanted to close so bad that I could hardly keep them open. There was only one thing to do.

I stood up. "Let's get this over with." I gave Lucas a hand to help her up off the couch, grabbed the key card to our own room, and led the way out the door.

When we got up to the sixth floor, the hall was empty and shadowy, and everything was very, very quiet. Paul and Teresa's huge suite was at the corner, the very last door on the right. Seneca's room was second to the end, and Edie's next to hers. That meant we had to pass Edie's room to get where we were going.

"What if somebody's sleeping in Seneca's room?" I whispered.

"Why would they be?"

"I don't know. But they could be."

I remembered our excuse, but somehow even if we used it, I knew we'd be in trouble. As we got closer to Edie's door, I kept expecting it to open. At last I could see her room number. Two more steps and we were even with it. I looked at the handle. Would it move suddenly downward? Would the door fly open? Would Edie march out and block our way, hands on her hips? My heart was beating so hard I was sure it could be heard outside my body, like the bass rhythm coming from a car with its stereo system turned way up.

But the door handle never moved and then, finally, we were past Edie's room. Three more quiet steps, and we were in front of Seneca's door.

Lucas put the card in the slot; there was a soft click. If someone was sleeping in Seneca's room, would it wake them? Paul and Teresa's bedroom was separated from Seneca's room by the sitting room, but what if both doors between them were open? The tiny light on the lock turned green. Lucas pressed down on the handle slowly, slowly, slowly. At last she silently eased the door open just far enough to peek in.

Her head turned to look from one side of the room to the other before she whispered, "It's okay," and stepped inside.

I tiptoed in and closed the door silently behind us. Then I sagged against the wall and let out a lungful of air. I wondered how long I'd been holding my breath.

The only light in the room came from the street outside, but the hall had been so dim that my eyes took only a few seconds to get used to the darkness. I looked over to the dresser where I'd left the phone. My heart sank.

Maybe it was just because of the shadows, but I was almost sure there was nothing on that dresser now.

Walking softly on the carpet, I crossed to take a closer look. No phone. Had it fallen off? I got down on the floor and felt around. It was nowhere.

Still on my knees, I turned to where Lucas was standing behind me.

"Not here," I breathed.

By the time I got back to my feet, she had moved a few steps away and was standing with her ear up against the door that connected Seneca's room with Edie's. She crooked her finger, gesturing for me to come over.

Beside her, I leaned up against the door and heard the low sound of a man's voice. Then, a minute later, one of Edie's too-loud laughs.

"If it's Paul, he'll come through this room," I whispered.

Lucas nodded and straightened. "Let's get out of here."

At that exact moment, the handle moved, brushing Lucas's arm, and the door swung toward us.

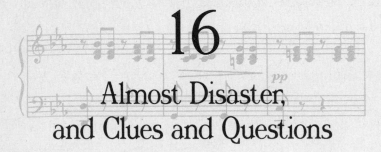

16

Almost Disaster, and Clues and Questions

Lucas jumped in my direction, and I gasped and took a quick step backward.

Part of a man's arm appeared. "I'll see you in the morning." Paul. Speaking softly.

One hand was at my mouth, the other was holding on to Lucas's arm for dear life. We were *sooooo* busted.

"Not so fast." Edie's usually loud voice was softer than I'd ever heard it. "Come back here. We're not finished."

Paul's arm disappeared, he moved back into Edie's room, and the door closed behind him.

"Quick, under the bed," Lucas whispered, and the two of us scrambled in from opposite sides, each fighting with the duvet.

Once safely in place, I didn't breathe, didn't move. I know Lucas didn't either, because we were holding each other's hands with a death grip. We lay that way, on our backs as stiff as chunks of frozen fish, until at last I felt Lucas's body sag a little and she let out a breath. I breathed, too, and we let go of hands. I felt like we'd just survived a near-death experience.

My heart had been pounding so loud in my ears that I probably wouldn't have heard a jet flying ten feet over my head. It must have taken most of a minute before I stopped hearing the sound of the blood whooshing through my veins.

I wondered how long it was going to be before Paul finished with Edie and came through so we could get back to our room, but mostly I wondered what he was doing in there with her at that time of night. Could they be having an affair? She wasn't nearly as good-looking as Teresa, but maybe Paul liked the tall blond type.

I wanted to ask Lucas about it then and there, but with the duvet blocking both our view of the door and some of the sound in the room, I wasn't sure we'd know when Edie's connecting door opened. Even the softest whispering seemed risky. Lucas must have thought the same thing. She stayed quiet, too.

All that excitement had made my tiredness go away. At least for a while. And that was good, because stuck there, it was the first time since Lucas and I had stood hugging each other and crying on Lothian Road that I'd had a chance to think.

I thought a little bit more about why Paul and Edie

might be together. And I thought about that surreal scene in the dressing room, from the moment when Paul and Edie and Teresa and Lucas and I were standing outside the artistes' suite waiting for Seneca to come to the door—was it really less than five hours ago?—all the way up until Lucas and I left with Edie. It was like a DVD that kept rerunning in my brain. And the difference between having it happen in the first place and thinking about it now was that I had time to go over every part separately.

It wasn't until I'd gone over the whole thing the third time that I started to wonder if maybe there were clues in what had happened. And when I went through everything again looking at it that way, I started to have some questions.

First, in those minutes after the kidnapping, why hadn't Paul or Edie cared that Lucas and I were standing there, and why hadn't they tried to get us out of the room *then*? Was I nuts, or had Paul only gotten mad about having us there when he found out Mom had left town? I wanted to talk this over with Lucas.

And now I remembered what I'd been reminded of when he blew his top: it was just like the way he had acted the first time I saw him, slamming that cell phone down on the table in the hotel coffee shop.

Another thing I thought of was the way the artistes' suite looked when I came back with Parker. Or, rather, the impression I had when I came into the room and saw everybody standing there, nobody moving. I'd had a feel-ing about it then, like when you smell something and you know it reminds you of another time or place, but you don't stop to figure out exactly what. So what *had* it re-minded me of?

It was probably more than a minute before I finally got it. It had reminded me of an Agatha Christie play I'd seen the year before. At the end of one of the scenes, somebody had come in to say they'd found a body or a clue or some-thing, I can't quite remember. Anyway, whatever it was, all the actors stopped moving and stood absolutely still like that for a minute until the curtain closed.

When I'd thought about that for a while, I started won-dering about this "dollhouse castle in the sky" Parker had talked about. It seemed ridiculous, but Parker wasn't lying. I could tell. Little kids make horrible liars.

So I was concentrating on this castle, whatever and wherever it was, and how we might get there, when Lucas's hand closed over my wrist, holding tight. I heard the sound of someone whispering (I couldn't tell what was said or even if it was a man or a woman talking), the click of a door closing, and a moment later, the much more quiet sound of the door closing on the other side of the room. Paul was being so careful not to wake Teresa that I hadn't heard one single footstep or any sound of the connecting door to their room when he'd opened it.

We lay there, not moving, not knowing if Paul might

think of something else he had to say to Edie and come back through.

Maybe three minutes passed before we heard the sound of a toilet being flushed in the bathroom off the sitting room.

"Let's go!" Lucas whispered.

Quickly, quietly, we scrambled out from under the bed and out the door. Once in the hall, we ran full speed to the door to the stairway and down the stairs as fast as we could.

"Holy meep!" Lucas exploded when we got back to our room. "What a day! What a night!" She was already kicking off her shoes and unbuttoning her blouse. "What do you think Paul and Edie were up to in that room? I can't believe they'd be, like, you know—"

I nodded. "I know what you mean."

"He's married to Teresa—he can't want to have something going with Edie, with her loud voice and way she has of acting so important. That would be weird."

Now she was scrambling in her suitcase for her pajamas. "Maybe she's blackmailing him. Like, 'Give me the money and I'll hand over Seneca.'"

She straightened up, her pajamas in her hands. "What's wrong? Why are you so quiet?"

By this time I was pulling my own pajama top over my head. "We need to go to the dollhouse castle in the sky, Lucas."

"We need to—" she stopped. "You've got one of your feelings?"

I nodded.

I'm not stupid. I get good grades and everything. But Lucas is way, way smarter than I am. The thing is, though, she doesn't have an intuition like I do, and she knows by now that when my intuition tells me something, she should take it seriously.

We were both quiet as we finished changing and got our toiletry bags out of our suitcases. Once in the bathroom, Lucas handed the toothpaste to me and I put some on my brush.

"Does your intuition tell you anything about where it is or what we'll do when we get there?" Lucas asked.

"Nope. At least not yet. All I know is that we need to go and look at the place."

I started brushing. Lucas was a little bit ahead of me. When she rinsed her mouth out, she said, "I've never been to a dollhouse castle in the sky before."

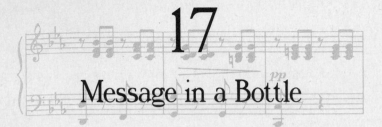

17
Message in a Bottle

"Kari!" Lucas was shaking me awake.

"What?"

"What's your mother's e-mail address?"

I rubbed my eyes and shook my head. It took my foggy brain a minute to remember it. At last I said, "G Welles PDQ at gmail dot com."

"Yeah, that's what I thought it was."

"Why? What's going on?" I looked at the clock. It was only ten past eight. I'd gotten less than six hours of sleep. No wonder I felt like throwing a pillow at Lucas, putting another over my head, and zoning out again.

I sat up, and the reality of the night before hit me like a brick: Seneca was gone, she and Parker were in danger, and we couldn't reach Mom.

"I've been using one of the computers in the lobby," Lucas said, "trying to break into your mom's Gmail account to see if she had messages from Celia with her cell phone number, or something about where they were going to stay in Inverness. But I couldn't make ten sixty-six work."

"Did you try ten sixty-six ten sixty-six?"

"Yes, and I tried every other combination of those numbers I could think of. Isn't that what she always uses for a password?"

"As far as I know. Did you send her a message?"

"Not yet."

"How long have you been up?"

"About an hour. I woke up when it got light out and I couldn't get back to sleep, thinking about . . . everything."

Everything. Yeah, there was a lot to think about that could keep a person awake. No wonder Lucas's voice sounded glum and tired and anxious.

"I even tried calling Robert's restaurant to see if he left some kind of number where he could be reached, but the message just said the place was closed for the annual summer vacation and would open up again a week from tomorrow night."

We'd stayed with Celia's friend Robert earlier in the summer when we were in London. He owned a restaurant, and right now he was in California on a wine-buying tour for restaurant owners.

"This all stinks," I muttered.

Lucas handed me a bag. "I brought you a scone. And

here's a cup of coffee. I know you're not all that crazy about it, but I thought it would help you wake up. As soon as possible I want to go wait at the door of the tourist information office. They don't open until nine, but there'll probably be a billion people in line because of Festival."

"Why do you want to go to the tourist office?" I was stirring sugar into my coffee. Lucas was right. I did need something to help my brain start working, but I'd rather it was a Coke. Whatever.

"I thought they might know what *dollhouse castle in the sky* means. I Googled it, but all I came up with was stuff about dolls."

I took the first sip. Too hot. I got out of bed and went to the little refrigerator for some ice, noticing as I went that it was raining outside. "Why not check with the person at the desk downstairs?"

"Because I don't want Paul or Edie to see me and ask the clerk what I wanted to know. They'll figure out we're gone at some point, but I want us to be out of town before they notice."

"Ah." It was all I could manage.

"I'll go down and start an e-mail message to your mom telling her what's happened. She's got to read her e-mail at some point. You'd think. If you could hurry to get ready, you could come downstairs and finish the message while I go off to the tourist office."

The ice cube had cooled the coffee. I took two big

swallows, and right away I felt more awake. "Yeah, that's fine. Go ahead. I'll be down in a couple minutes."

In fact it only took about five minutes for me to wash my face, brush my teeth, comb my hair, and throw on my jeans and a T-shirt and a hoodie. As I waited for the elevator, scarfing down the last bite of the scone, I wondered if Lucas might have taken a minute to write to Josh, or if she'd have a message from him in her account. I doubted she'd hear from him.

I also wondered if Mom actually would read her e-mail at some point, like Lucas had said. Why would she, when we were supposed to have her stupid phone? What a mess! Sending her an e-mail message was a little like being stranded on a desert island and sending off a message in a bottle, hoping someone would get it and read it. Before it was too late.

I took the last sip of my coffee just as the elevator reached the ground floor, and a minute later I was sitting in the chair next to Lucas at the little row of computers in the lobby.

"That was fast," she said.

"How far have you gotten?" I asked, looking at the e-mail message on the screen.

I was on her left. With hardly any movement at all, she gestured with her head and eyes to the guy typing away at the computer on her right, as if to tell me she wasn't going to say anything that he could hear.

"See for yourself," she said.

The last line of her message to Mom started a new paragraph. It read:

There was a note on the piano that said Seneca had been kidnapped, and

"Okay," I said. "I'll take it from there. You go get in line at the tourist office."

"See you in a few," she said, and slipped off her chair.

Before she was even across the lobby, I was reading through what Lucas had written. She'd done a good job telling the story up to that point, using whole words and sentences like for a school paper, not the texting she and I do all the time. I supposed it had to be done that way because it was so long and complicated. Besides, we'd never hear the end of it from Mom if we didn't use proper English with her. I took a big breath, and launched in where Lucas had left off, typing as fast as I could.

I wrote about how upset Teresa was, about Paul and Edie getting mad at us, about Parker and what he saw, how worried we were about him, and how we'd gotten him to play the game of not telling any grownups what had happened. I wrote about our visit to Seneca's room the night before, and what we'd heard. I wrote about the things I'd thought of while I was under the bed.

Finally, I wrote:

Mom, no matter what happens, please, please, please don't say anything about this to Paul or Teresa or Edie, because it might not be safe for Parker, or for Seneca, or even for Lucas and me. And it occurred to me this morning that Paul or Edie or somebody might be using your phone to send text messages to Celia's phone pretending they're from me, and saying everything is fine. So if Celia's gotten any text messages saying things are like normal, that's just a plain lie.

Right now Lucas is standing in line at the tourist office to find out if somebody knows what "the dollhouse castle in the sky" means. When we find out, we'll probably go there. And we'll keep writing e-mail messages when we can. I miss you! I wish you were here. I've never wished you were here so much in my entire life.

Love,
Kari

And with that I sent our message in a bottle and logged off.

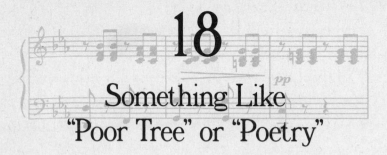

18
Something Like
"Poor Tree" or "Poetry"

Lucas was the fourth person in line, standing in the drizzle outside the tourist office, the hood of her sweatshirt up. I had just gotten up to her when they opened the door.

Fortunately there were a lot of people behind the counter to answer questions, so we got a clerk right away. He was an older guy, broad and a little overweight, with white hair and beard, and wire-rimmed glasses perched on his nose. His name tag said JOCK. Funny, he didn't look like a jock at all.

"Guid morning." A big Scottish accent. "How can I help ye bonnie lassies?"

Thank goodness Lucas was doing the talking. If it had been me, I'd have totally babbled, not knowing where to start. But Lucas being Lucas, she launched into it.

"We have kind of a weird question. Here in Scotland, what does *dollhouse castle in the sky* mean?"

"Dollhouse castle in the sky?" he repeated. "Where did you hear this?"

"From a little boy we know."

He fingered his beard for a minute, thinking. "He said *in the sky,* not *on sky?*"

"Why would it be *on* sky?" Lucas asked.

"Because we have a big island here called the Isle of Skye. The lad could have been talking about Old Dalhousie Castle on the Isle of Skye."

The name of the castle sounded almost like *dollhouse,* at least like a Scot would say it, with an *ie* at the end. I looked at Lucas. "That's got to be it! Remember how Parker said it might be a *little* dollhouse? That would be like *dollhousie.*" I turned to Jock. "Is it near here?"

Jock brought out a map of Scotland and started unfolding it. "There *is* a Dalhousie Castle not far from Edinburgh. But that's relatively modern. It wasn't begun until the fifteenth century." He looked at us with his eyes twinkling, to see if we got his joke, while he smoothed the map out in front of us and reached for a pencil. "There was a stronghold on the site of Old Dalhousie Castle on Skye at least three centuries before that.

"We're just here." He circled Edinburgh on the map in the southern part of Scotland on the east coast. "And here's the Isle of Skye." He pointed to a big island kitty-corner across the country, way up off the northwest coast, then circled a symbol, like a medieval tower, on the east side of the island, above a town called Portree. "This is the site of Old Dalhousie Castle."

He reached under the desk for a brochure called *Scotland's Castles*, leafed through it, finally found the right page, and turned it toward us. Sure enough, at the top it said, OLD DALHOUSIE CASTLE.

The castle didn't look anything like Edinburgh Castle except that it was very old and dark and cold-looking. Instead of a big, bright, light-colored castle with pretty little round, pointy roofs sticking up like you might see in a kids' book, this was a plain building with little slits for windows, taller than it was wide, made of stone so ancient it had turned almost black, built on a point of land that stuck out into the sea. Around it stood a thick stone wall with cutout parts spaced evenly around the top, kind of like widely separated teeth. You see them a lot in pictures and drawings of medieval castles. Walls like that are called battlements, which I only knew because I'd heard them talked about in this documentary about the Middle Ages that Mom had been watching once on the History Channel.

In the picture on the brochure, the sky was blue with a few lavender clouds, the sea was perfectly calm and almost purple, there was a patch of flowers in the grass—purple flowers of course—and the sun was shining on the castle and the enormous bluff in the background. Even with all this cheer around, Old Dalhousie Castle looked like a harsh and lonely place. I thought of Seneca being kept there—maybe when the sky was gray, and big, dark waves were crashing in. And castles had dungeons. I remembered the dungeon we'd visited at Edinburgh Castle—another castle that didn't look like it came out of a fairy tale—and I shivered.

"The place was abandoned a couple of centuries ago," Jock was saying, "But I've heard tell"—he pronounced this like *haired* tell—"it's been purchased and is under renovation."

"Who bought it?" Lucas asked.

"I think it was a MacDonald—or mebbe it was a MacLeod—who went to Australia and made a packet. Now he's back with enough money to build a fine family home near the site of the old clan. There have always been MacDonalds and MacLeods on Skye."

"How do we get there?" Lucas asked.

"When do you want to go?"

"Today."

Jock was looking from one of us to the other. "Michty me!" It sounded a little like *mick-tee* me. "And your families . . ." He let it trail off.

"Um, we're traveling with my mother," I said. "We're getting the information for her."

"Oh, aye?" He looked suspicious, sighed as if he was giving up, and turned to a computer screen. "I'll take a bit of a peep at the railway timetable. It's a long trip, and you may have to change trains."

He spent a few minutes with the mouse and the keyboard before turning back to us.

"Can you make a train at ten oh-five?"

Lucas looked up at the clock and I looked at my watch. We had a little more than fifty minutes. We nodded.

"Then it's nae sae bad." I figured he meant *not so bad*.

He jotted a few notes on a piece of paper, handed it to us, and explained our schedule. We had to catch a train from Waverley Station, which was underground directly downstairs from where we were standing. He told us about the stairway on Princes Street that led down to it, which we'd seen at least a dozen times.

"You'll be changing trains in Inverness," he said.

I burst out, "Inverness! That's where—" I was going to say that that's where Mom was, but remembered just in time that we'd told him we were getting this information for her. "That's where some friends of ours live." I tried to sound as confident as I could, hoping Jock wouldn't get suspicious. "How long will we be there?"

"Nearly two hours," he said.

Fat lot of good that would do. Like Mom would be walking around the station in Inverness just when we were there. Right.

Jock was continuing. "The train completes its journey at a place called Kyle of Lochalsh"—he pronounced the last word sort of like *lawk-AHLSH*—"at six twenty-two. You'll be takin' a bus from there at seven forty. And exactly one hour later," Jock finished, "it arrives at Portree. Do you need a hotel reservation?"

"Yes," Lucas answered. "We'll need—"

Something was ringing a bell in my mind. I put a hand on Lucas's arm. "Excuse me," I interrupted. "How did you pronounce the name of the town where we'll be staying?"

"Portree," he repeated. With his Scottish accent, it sounded something like *poor tree* or *poetry*.

Lucas said, "Kari, maybe it would be a good idea for you to go back to the hotel and pack while I finish here and go down and get our tickets."

I had something I was bursting to say to her, but I looked at the clock. There was no time. "Right. Um, I'll go back and *tell Mom*," I emphasized, "we have to pack in a hurry."

Lucas nodded. "I'll meet you at the train."

"I—we'll be there as soon as we possibly can. Lucas, I have something extremely important to tell you about. You will not meeping believe it."

She raised her eyebrows. "It'll have to wait."

"Thank you, Jock," I said, turned, and walked fast across the room.

Before I got out the door, I heard her say, "And about the hotel. We'll need a room for three, for two nights. And you can guarantee it with this credit card number." As usual, she seemed to know exactly what she was doing. Back out in the rain, I reminded myself that even though being rich doesn't buy happiness, it has its advantages. Like Lucas having her own credit card.

I had to work hard to concentrate on packing, because my mind was so full of what I'd figured out about Seneca's kidnapping. Just when I got my suitcase packed with everything we'd need, it occurred to me that if Paul or Edie saw me wheeling it through the lobby, they'd know Lucas and I were traveling somewhere, and we didn't want that. So I weeded out a few things and stuffed what we absolutely had to have into my backpack and a plastic shopping bag. Later, we could transfer the things from the plastic bag into Lucas's backpack, which she had with her.

On my way out I passed the little row of computers and realized I needed to send another e-mail to Mom telling her where we were going—I wished I'd waited to find out the name of our hotel in Portree—and what I'd figured out that morning. I did that as fast as I could, then headed back out into the rain, darting around people, running when I could, across the long bridge and down the staircase that led from Princes Street to Waverley Station.

What with all the delays, I was cutting the time really close. Lucas was waiting for me at the bottom of the stairs, dancing up and down in nervousness. "Come on or we're going to miss our train! This way!"

We ran across the station to a gate where she showed our tickets to a guard, and walked through to the platform where our train was sitting. We hopped on the very first carriage we came to, and the train started moving right away.

For some reason, we didn't think to look back at the crowd in the station to see if anyone was watching us. We should have.

19

It Falls into Place

We grabbed on to a nearby luggage rack to keep our balance as the train moved out of the station.

"Okay, what's the deal?" Lucas said. "I've been dying to know what you have to tell me!"

It took me a second to catch my breath—I was panting from all the hurrying I'd done. Finally I started in, talking softly so the people around wouldn't hear me. "Okay. You remember what I said about seeing Paul that morning in the hotel, when he got all mad and slammed his cell phone down?"

Lucas nodded.

"Remember I said the clerk helped him, and Paul didn't even say thanks?"

She nodded again.

"Well, what the clerk was helping him with was using the telephone code he needed to make his call. Guess where he was calling." With an imitation Scottish accent, I said, "Portree."

"Ho . . . ly . . . schmack."

I let the news sink in.

"So it's for sure that Paul's in on it with Edie," she said at last.

We walked forward in the train, going through three more crowded cars before we found some empty seats facing forward across a little table from a big guy who was sprawled sound asleep over both the backward-facing seats.

I threw our luggage onto the overhead rack while Lucas scooted in beside the window. I fell in beside her. We were both sitting half turned so we could look at each other while we talked. It seemed like, with this clue, we were beginning to make sense of Seneca's kidnapping.

"But *why* would Paul want to kidnap his own stepdaughter?" I said. "I mean, why would you want to pay a ransom to yourself with your own family's money?"

"You're right. It doesn't make any sense. Unless he wants to leave Teresa," Lucas said.

"They seem pretty happy together to me."

"Yeah, but I don't think you can ever tell for sure," Lucas said. She dug around in her backpack and brought out two bottles of orange juice and handed one to me. "You hungry? I bought some sandwiches and things in the station."

I shook my head. I noticed, looking through the window as she leaned over to put her backpack down, that the sun had come out, most of Edinburgh was behind us, and we were on the longest bridge I'd ever seen, going over water that led out into the sea.

Lucas took a sip of her OJ, set it down on the little table in front of our seats, and turned to see what I was looking at. "This must be the Firth of Forth," she said, almost like she was muttering to herself.

"What?"

"The Firth of Forth," she said in a more normal voice. "I think *firth* means something like *fjord*. Sort of like a big cut in the side of the land where the sea comes in."

This was just one of those billion things Lucas always seemed to know about, and at that moment I didn't care. I just wanted to talk about Seneca. And Paul. And Edie. I wanted us to go over all the questions and all the clues and see what we could figure out.

"So if Edie's in on it and Paul's in on it," I said, skipping over all the firths and forths and fjords, "that answers at least one of my questions."

"What questions?"

I took a sip from my juice. "Last night, when we were lying there in Seneca's room waiting for Paul, I thought of a couple things. And one thing was the way the artistes' suite looked when I walked into it with Parker."

I told her about the Agatha Christie play, and how

all the actors had frozen in place at the end of one of the scenes. "That's what it reminded me of, Lucas. A play. And I think it *was* like a play.

"I think Paul and Edie had it all planned out, exactly how it would happen. We'd all be waiting outside the suite for Seneca to answer the door. Finally one of us would open the door, and bingo—no Seneca. Paul would walk across the room and find the ransom note on the piano. They probably knew Teresa would start to cry—what mother wouldn't if she found out her kid had been kidnapped? Edie would move over to comfort her; it was all planned out."

Lucas thought about this. "Who was the audience supposed to be?"

"All I can think of is that it was supposed to be *Mom*! And Lucas, I think that's why Paul was so mad when he found out she wasn't there!"

"Why would he want her to be there?"

"Because he wanted her to write a story about it?" I made it into a question, and shrugged while I was saying it, because I wasn't sure that *was* why.

I turned and stared out the window. There was a goose perched in the middle of a field surrounded by a stone fence. In the distance, puffy clouds looked like they were actually sitting on the sea.

I thought about Paul being in on Seneca's kidnapping. Even though he'd been so charming when we met him, and Seneca had said he was getting her mom and Edie to treat her better, I'd had a bad feeling about Paul from the minute I saw him in the coffee shop. Sure enough, I'd been right. This might have been partly intuition, but it was also because it seemed to me only selfish people had the kind of temper tantrum Paul had had.

The train slowed as we pulled into a little town that I think was pretty, although I hardly noticed it because I had so much on my mind. Lucas turned to glance out at the small gray wooden station house and the sign that said Inverkeithing, then turned back toward me.

"What *I* was thinking about while we were under the bed was how many times in the last few days somebody's said or noticed something about the color green. First there's Mr. Green Socks. Plus, do you remember, when Seneca was looking through the binoculars, she mentioned something about Edie talking to a guy wearing a green striped shirt?"

"Yeah, I remember. The cab driver."

"She said he *must* be a cab driver, so she didn't know it for sure."

"Oh, and Lucas, do you remember when we were first watching Seneca's rehearsal and I thought I saw that flash of green in the balcony? I'll bet it was a man in a green shirt after all!"

A few seconds passed as we thought about all this, then I said, "There was another green thing, Lucas. When we were watching those comedians, Scotty and Scotty, did you notice the two guys on the other side of the stage who—"

I broke off, caught my breath, and grabbed her arm. "Lucas, they were the kidnappers!" My heart was pounding as I put it all together. "Those two guys! Did you see them standing across from us looking at Seneca?"

Lucas shook her head, but then she got that faraway look that sometimes means she's going through her mind's hard drive for a picture. She must have found it, because suddenly her eyes got huge. "You're right!" she said. "One of them was wearing a green shirt. With stripes."

"Green and white stripes. Who knows—maybe he was wearing green socks to match his shirt. And he had a head covered in stubble, like what Parker said about Green Socks! And Lucas, the other one was dark and had a big mustache, just like the baker—"

"In *My Neighborhood Book*!" we both finished together.

"I'll bet you money Green Socks is the same guy Seneca saw talking to Edie on that bridge!" Lucas said, her eyes almost blazing. "That's how Seneca knew Edie was in on it! It's all falling into place."

20

Clues, Deductions, and Doing Away with What's-Her-Name

At the next station, the big guy who'd been sprawled across from us got out, and a couple got into our car and came down the aisle in our direction. They both had gray hair. The woman was plump and wore an awful nylon pink sweatshirt kind of thing with flowers all over it, and green polyester pants that matched the leaves on the flowers. The guy had a huge gut that hung out over his khakis.

"Here are some free seats, Frank," the woman said, and pointed at the seats across from us. She had an American voice so loud it was almost a yell.

It took them a couple of minutes to get settled, but when they did, we were looking straight at Frank and What's-Her-Name, and they were about four feet away looking at us.

Lucas and I shot each other a glance. Great. We couldn't talk about Seneca's kidnapping right in front of them. And there weren't any empty seats—there were people walking back and forth from car to car with their suitcases, looking for places to sit.

The woman fished around in her huge purse, pulled out a guidebook, and set it in front of her.

"Look at the purple flowers," she shouted as the train started up again. "That's heather, Frank! Isn't that interesting?" She pronounced it *in-ter-esting*.

I looked out the window. Sure enough, there were patches of lavender flowers by the tracks and, for that matter, dotting the fields in the distance. I remembered that before our trip, Mom had said something about heather in Scotland.

We were picking up speed. Lucas made a little gesture with her head toward Frank and What's-Her-Name and moved in closer to me.

"By the way," she said softly, "I figured your mom probably called the Fair Camellia to tell her that you and I were staying in Edinburgh while she went to Inverness, and to give her the phone numbers where she could be reached. So I found a phone at Waverley Station and left a message on Mom's cell asking her to send that stuff to us in an e-mail."

"That was brilliant, Lucas!" I said. "We should have thought of that last night!"

"Don't get your hopes up," she said in a grim voice. "Mom went up to that same place last year, one of the times I was staying with you—don't you remember? She only called me once in the whole four days she was gone, when they went to a different part of the island for dinner, because the cabin was out of cell phone range."

I sighed. I did remember. I told Lucas about sending the second e-mail to Mom.

"The way our luck is going," she said, "neither of our mothers will pick up their messages for days."

"Frank, it says here that the Macbeth in Shakespeare's play was a real Scottish king, and the castle where he lived was right outside of Inverness. Isn't that in-ter-est-ing?"

"Oh, meep," Lucas muttered, rolling her eyes at Frank and What's-Her-Name.

I got out of my seat, reached up to my backpack in the overhead rack, fished out my journal and two pencils, sat back down, and wrote, *Not only do we have to listen to What's-Her-Name screaming, we can't talk about all the things we just figured out!*

Lucas reached for the journal and a pencil and wrote, *Write about them.*

I wrote, *Make a list?* and showed this to Lucas. She nodded. I chewed on my pencil for a while. What I wrote next was kind of in shorthand, but translated into whole sentences it said, *Let's start with our deductions and work backward to the clues. Like thinking Seneca was telling us Edie was in on the kidnapping because she dropped the Queen of Swords card for Parker to pick up.*

A translation of Lucas's shorthand said, *And she had told us the Queen of Swords on the card looked like Edie.*

Me: *Good. Your turn.*

Lucas: *Why did Seneca think Edie was in on it? Because the guy waiting in her dressing room to kidnap Seneca turned out to be the guy with the green shirt Edie was talking to when Seneca was looking out the window with our opera glasses.*

We kept this up, writing a few more clues and deductions about the guy in green. When we got to the part about the guy I'd seen in the balcony, I wrote, *By the way, I think that's why he and Mustache were staring at Seneca during the Scotty and Scotty show. How much do you want to bet Edie or Paul let them into the Usher Hall so they could get a good look at her?*

Lucas: *And check out the artistes' suite.*

Me: *And the violin crate.*

We'd gotten this far when What's-Her-Name yelled, "Frank, it says here that Glasgow is Scotland's biggest city, but Edinburgh is the capital. Isn't that in-ter-esting?"

I wrote, *Do you think anyone would notice if you held What's-Her-Name down while I stuck a gag in her mouth?*

Lucas wrote, *If we have to put up with this woman all the way to Inverness, our trip to Skye had better not turn out to be a wild goose chase.*

I glanced at Lucas, wondering if she was mad at me for getting her to go on this trip, but she was saving all her dirty looks for What's-Her-Name. That was a relief.

It was bad enough heading up to Portree without knowing for sure that was where Seneca was being held. What with all the stuff that was happening—the worry, the lack of sleep, and everything—the last thing I needed was to have Lucas make me feel responsible if we didn't find Seneca where we hoped we would.

Maybe to make myself feel like we *weren't* on a wild goose chase, I got us started writing down our clues and deductions about the dollhouse castle in the sky. That led to the part about Paul's call to Portree, and the late-night meeting Paul and Edie had had in her room while we hid under the bed.

About that time, What's-Her-Name found something else to yell about. "Frank, it says here that a lot of Scots are such fans of soccer teams, which they call football clubs, that they wear their clubs' uniforms all the time and get in fights with fans from other clubs. Isn't that in-ter-esting?"

Lucas grabbed the journal, turned to a back page, made a quick sketch of What's-Her-Name, drew a big circle around it, then made one diagonal line through it, like one of those PROHIBITED signs.

It made me smile. But my mind was busy thinking about what What's-Her-Name had said.

I took the journal and, under the WHAT'S-HER-NAME PROHIBITED sign I wrote, *Was that what the green was about? Soccer uniforms?*

Lucas wrote, *Let's look it up when we can get on the Internet.* Then she flipped back to the page we'd been writing on before. *What makes us think Paul wanted your mom to be there when the kidnapping happened? Because Paul acted mad when he found out your mom was gone and we'd been left behind.*

Me: *Also because of my feeling about the Agatha Christie play, which isn't exactly enough of a clue to put in a list.*

Lucas and I kept writing notes to each other. We were running out of things we'd figured out, so we started in on things we weren't sure about. Like, why did Paul want Mom to be there to see the scene in the artistes' suite? And were Paul and Edie lovers? And why would Paul be trying to get a ransom from his own family?

About that time, What's-Her-Name started in again. "Frank, it says here that Prince Charles and Camilla spend a lot of their time in Scotland at their place near Balmoral Castle. Isn't that in-ter-esting?"

Lucas and I rolled our eyes and sighed. I looked back down at the page, tried to forget about What's-Her-Name, and got us going on a list of some of the things we knew for sure, and things we'd heard, like what Parker said about Seneca being put in an instrument crate and hauled off in the back of a truck.

Sometime while we were in the middle of doing this we got hungry, so we each took one of the sandwiches Lucas had gotten for us when she was in the train station, and we bought a Coke and a couple of Kit Kat bars from a young guy who came through with a food cart.

When we finished, our clues and deductions and questions and other random facts and ideas were spread over seven of the sheets in my journal, and they were a mess, with arrows and smiley and frowny faces and some erasing. So we pulled the sheets out and, working together—me writing, Lucas pointing—we came up with an organized list with all the clues numbered, and our deductions listed with the numbers of the clues beside them. I'm not going to include it because it would be way too boring to read. But I felt better when it was done. Not because the seven pages had been a mess, but because my *thinking* had been a mess. The new, cleaned-up list had helped me get my thoughts about the kidnapping all tidied up and organized, like picking up my room when it gets way over-the-top messy. (Which I don't do often enough, according to Mom.)

During this whole time, the woman across from us read about a hundred more in-ter-esting things to Frank from her guidebook. Like that most Scots don't like the English. And that the Scottish people are divided up into clans, or families, and every clan has its own tartan plaid design.

I think it was after that one that I wrote, *How about we do away with What's-Her-Name?*

Lucas: *I've got just the right way: smother her with that meeping guidebook!*

Me: *In-ter-esting!* ☺

This all helped take our minds off things, but we weren't laughing like you'd think we would be, because of course Seneca was still trapped in the castle. Every so often as I wrote, I'd think about her.

When we were done with our lists, Lucas pulled her iPod out of her backpack and fell asleep with music blasting in her ears so loud that I could actually hear it, and didn't wake up even with What's-Her-Name shouting.

I kept thinking about Seneca, hoping we would find her at Old Dalhousie Castle, and that we could find a way to rescue her. I couldn't wait to get to the Isle of Skye and get started. Waiting was killing me.

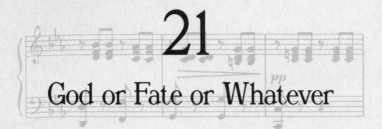

21
God or Fate or Whatever

Eventually Frank did the whole train car a favor and fell asleep. And without What's-Her-Name yelling into my face every minute and a half, I finally fell asleep, too.

When I woke up, the scenery had changed. I figured we must have gotten to the Highlands. We were surrounded by mountains, but instead of being covered with trees, like most of the mountains I was used to, these were covered in nothing but grass and lots and lots and lots and lots of heather. I'd never seen so much of anything in my life. Everywhere I looked, the fields and hills were either purple with it, or they were kind of a rusty color where the heather that had been there had died. There were hardly any houses around, but there seemed to be a lot of sheep, some of them with long black faces and longer ears than the sheep in Minnesota. The sky was always moving, the clouds rushing around, sometimes covering the sun and sometimes letting the sun shine through.

Lucas was still asleep, the music still blaring. But it wasn't more than ten minutes before I started seeing buildings, the train slowed down, and What's-Her-Name said, "Wake up, Frank. We're coming into Inverness." I was amazed she didn't say this was "in-ter-esting."

I woke Lucas, and we started getting our stuff together, her yawning the whole time. At last we got out of the train and into the station, and Frank and What's-Her-Name went into a little restaurant, maybe saving Lucas and me from spending time behind bars for assault.

We walked outside and discovered that we were smack in the middle of a busy part of Inverness. We talked about wandering around to see if we could run into Mom, but that didn't seem very likely. We decided to try calling hotels instead. So we found two pay phones and started calling every hotel in the phone book. But there were hundreds of them—way more than we ever would have guessed—and it seemed like we spent an awful lot of time on hold. So we'd only gotten to the ones that started with *O* when our time in Inverness was running out and we had to buy some more food and get back on the train. It made us even more discouraged than we'd been before, which was already pretty discouraged.

We got some more sandwiches and some potato chips, which the Scottish call *crisps*. To drink we got Irn-Bru—

they pronounced it like *iron brew*—a bright orange Scottish soft drink with an odd flavor that we both kind of liked.

When we were sitting on the train waiting to leave the station, I said, "Lucas, I know I was the one who felt like we had to get to the dollhouse castle in the sky to help rescue Seneca. But I still don't know what we should do when we get there. Do you have any ideas?"

"Not really." Her voice sounded the most depressed it had been so far. "What I guess I was hoping was that somehow we'd get hold of your mom and she could help us plan what to do next."

Just for a minute I let myself think about how nice it would be if Mom were there to help us. But I ended up saying, "I think we're going to have to plan it on our own."

"Is this because of your intuition?"

"Not just my intuition. I was thinking about this earlier. About how hard we've tried to get a message to Mom, and we're not any closer to getting hold of her now than we were to begin with.

"Remember what you said about my mom or your mom getting our messages?" I continued. "Something about 'the way our luck is going'? Well, I'm not sure it's just bad luck, Lucas. Because if it is, we're having an awful lot of it."

I expected Lucas to interrupt me, but instead she kept looking at me. Not like she was mocking, but like she was really interested. So I kept talking.

"I mean, think of all the things that have happened just

the right way, or the *wrong* way, so we can't get in touch with Mom. First she decides to leave with Celia after the concert intermission. The second thing was when I left the phone in Seneca's room."

Lucas nodded.

"And you and I could have been listening when Mom told Teresa the name of the hotel where she and Celia would be staying in Inverness, but we weren't. And then Mom didn't use ten sixty-six as her password for her Gmail account. And if she was telling the truth to Teresa, she's not checking her e-mails. And *your* mom, who might have Celia's cell phone number or the name of the hotel where Mom and Celia are staying, is on Madeline Island in Lake Superior, out of cell phone range."

The doors closed on the train, and we started moving out of the station. "Well, what I'm wondering is if God or fate or whatever is keeping us from getting in touch with Mom. Or, actually, keeping Mom away from the whole Seneca kidnapping thing."

"God? Or fate?"

"Or a higher power or the universe or something. I know you're not big on believing in that kind of thing—"

"It's not that I don't believe. It's just that I don't know," Lucas said.

"Whatever. But think about this, Lucas. All those things that kept us from getting hold of Mom—that can't just be coincidence."

She sat and looked out as the train started going faster.

"So if God or fate or whatever doesn't want your mom in on this, why not? Do you think it's about her—your mom, I mean? Or about us?"

"Maybe it's about Seneca," I said. "Or maybe it has something to do with who'll get punished."

"We'll probably never know."

"Maybe not." But somehow I thought we'd probably end up knowing the answer before many more days went by.

22

The Isle of Skye

"I wonder what Josh would think about all this."

It was the first thing Lucas had said about Josh for almost exactly twenty-four hours. If it weren't for the whole Seneca-kidnapping thing, Lucas's silence about Josh would have made it one of the best twenty-four-hour periods I'd spent in a long time. Yeah, I was sorry she even said this much. But it was way better than it could have been.

All day long I'd been expecting her to come up with something like, "I wonder if he senses, somewhere deep inside himself, that I am moving ever closer to peril?" Or, "If only he were here and we could rely on his extraordinary strength and intelligence!" But instead, she was just wondering what he'd think. I was shocked!

We were finally on the Isle of Skye, on the bus that had taken us from Kyle of Lochalsh, where the train tracks had ended, across another hugely long bridge leading over the sea to the island. Now we were on a road winding around hills that might even have been higher and barer—if *barer* is a word—than the ones we'd already passed through. All the road signs were in English, with a translation below in another language, which Lucas said was probably Gaelic, an old language some people still use in Scotland. There were even fewer houses here than on the mainland. Those that were here were pretty much all white or gray and all alone, with no trees around them like they'd have if they were in America. Nothing to protect them from the wind. The sun was getting low in the sky, and the evening was made almost dark by the fast-moving clouds and a little rain off and on.

It all seemed very lonely, even to me, sitting next to my best friend. Assuming Seneca actually was at Old Dalhousie Castle—and of course we didn't know that for sure—I thought about how much lonelier it must seem to her, with a view of bare hills, and the wind maybe whistling through the cracks. The weather was a lot cooler up here. Our hoodies weren't quite warm enough—the people on the bus were all wearing sweaters or jackets. Was Seneca cold? Parker said that when she was kidnapped she'd been wearing her hoodie over her concert dress, and all she'd taken was her stuffed bunny. Did she have a furnace to keep her room warm, or a fire in a fireplace? I shivered, and pulled my sweatshirt closer around me. And I had that dungeon thought again, which almost made me sick. I'd decided not to tell Lucas about the dungeon because I didn't want her being sick thinking about it, too.

I'd also wondered a lot about Parker, both on the train trip and now on the way to Portree. What if he didn't keep the secret? If he told his parents, and they told Paul. . . I couldn't even stand to think about that.

Lucas's comment about Josh, even though I wished she hadn't mentioned him, was at least a break from all these depressing things. In my opinion, the answer to her question about what he would think about this was something like: *Meep Seneca. Where can I find a video game?*

Of course I couldn't say that to Lucas. Still, I thought I might as well give a nudge in the right direction. So I said, "Do you think he'd be as interested as we are? He strikes me as kind of a, uh, happy-go-lucky guy," *happy-go-lucky* being the closest I could come to *Josh Daniels is about as deep and interesting as your average mud puddle.*

I knew what was coming next. Sure enough. "Well, he has that gift of laughter."

I wanted to groan. But this time when she said it, her face didn't get that goofy look. There was something new there. Was she not quite as enthused about Josh as she had been? Had she suddenly realized that the last thing we needed right then was a smart-meep? That a "gift of laughter" might have its limits?

The rest of our trip into Portree was mostly quiet. The naps on the train had helped us make up for the sleep we'd missed the night before, but we were still tired from the long, long trip. Plus we'd pretty much said everything we had to say.

It was a short walk from the bus stop to our hotel. We'd expected some trouble when we tried to check in without a parent, but it went so well it was amazing. The desk clerk was a beautiful blonde not too many years older than we were, with a different accent—we found out later she was from Poland—and she also had to take care of the customers at a little bar in the corner, so she was too busy to pay much attention to us. When Lucas told her that my mother would be arriving the next day, she just shrugged her shoulders, said something about asking the manager, and had us sign in.

When we finished at the desk, we stopped at the one computer they had in the hotel lobby and checked both my e-mail and Lucas's. No messages from our mothers. No surprise. We sent Mom a message telling her the name of our hotel, then went up to our room. I happened to notice when we were looking for messages from Mom in Lucas's in-box that she didn't have any from Josh either.

The hotel was a nice place, on a hill looking over the Portree harbor. Our room was one floor up. I don't know when I've seen a more awesome view. A row of pastel-colored two-story buildings stood lined up along the water, the first one yellow, then a green one, a blue one, and a pink one. Behind them was a stone church, a little hill with trees, and some kind of a ruin. The sun had just set, and the colors of the sky matched the colors of the buildings.

It almost seemed like a sign that everything was going to turn out all right. That Parker would be safe and we'd be able to rescue Seneca after all, even if we had to do it ourselves.

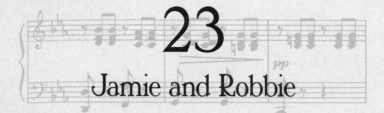

23
Jamie and Robbie

There were still no e-mail messages from either of our mothers in the morning. While we were at the computer, we looked up the Scottish soccer teams—or, as What's-Her-Name said they called them, football clubs. I thought maybe the club's name was Carling because I remembered the word on the front of the shirt Green Socks was wearing. But when we Googled "Carling football club" we found out Carling was the name of a beer that sponsored a lot of sports teams. We gave that up and tried "Scottish football club green," and with a couple more clicks there we were, looking at a football jersey just like the one I'd seen on Green Socks. It was the Celtic club, from Glasgow. It turned out they were the club for the Catholics. Protestants rooted for another club called the Rangers. I'd never heard of athletic teams mixed up with religion before. Okay, so what good was it going to do us to know that Green Socks was a Celtic fan or a Catholic?

This was the kind of hotel where breakfast is included in the price, and there was a small breakfast room with people sitting at a few of the ten or twelve tables. A good-looking guy who was at least four inches over six feet and maybe about twenty years old directed us to a table by the window. He said his name was Jamie. He handed us menus and gave us a chance to look them over before he came back to get our orders. We both said we wanted scrambled eggs, bacon, and toast.

"No haggis?" Jamie said with a smile when we finished ordering. It was a nice smile, and I noticed he had curly hair the color of sand, and big blue eyes with long lashes.

"What's haggis?" I asked.

"Have ye nae haird about the haggis, then?" he said, those blue eyes twinkling. I noticed that his accent emphasized the *s* sound at the end of *haggis*.

We both shook our heads.

"It is a ground meat with oatmeal that we have in Scotland. If you are to have a real Scottish breakfast, you must be ordering the haggis."

"I'll try some," I said.

"Me, too," Lucas said in a whispery voice, and gave him a spaced-out kind of smile.

"Right-char then," Jamie said, and disappeared through the door into the kitchen.

"He's kind of cute. I love the way he talks!" I said.

Lucas nodded, and—I couldn't believe it—blushed. Blushed! Lucas! The only other time I'd ever seen her blush was the first time Josh had talked to her. Something was definitely going on.

I acted like I didn't notice, and got up to get us some orange juice from a side table with juices and cereals and things on it. If she was getting a thing for somebody besides Josh meeping Daniels, I sure didn't want to wreck it by teasing her about it.

When I got back, I said, "This morning when I was getting into the shower, you said you'd thought of something you wanted to tell me when we got to breakfast."

"Um, yeah." Lucas stared at me and blinked, as if her thoughts had been far away. It took her a minute to pull herself together, then she looked around the room, made sure no one was close enough to hear her, and said in a low voice, "I woke up once in the night and had an idea about why Paul would want to get a ransom from his own family."

"Which is. . . ."

"Which is, what if it's not actually the family's money? What if it's Seneca's money?"

"What's the difference?"

"Do you remember a few months ago when I told you I'd heard my parents arguing about my dad's will?"

"Yeah, sort of." Lucas's parents argued about so many things, it was hard to keep all their fights straight.

"Well, from what I overheard, Dad had decided that when he died, almost all of his money would go into something called a *trust* for Justin and me, and the Fair Camellia was going ballistic about this. I didn't know why, so I did some Googling about what a trust is. It turned out that whatever money Dad left in the trust for Justin and me was money Mom couldn't get her hands on. So she couldn't spend it."

I could see why Allen the Meep would want to leave some money the Fair Camellia couldn't spend. There was nothing in the world she did as well as spend money. Still, it didn't seem fair to leave almost *all* his money that way. But then, there was a reason we called him Allen the Meep.

"And I remember reading that there are a lot of different kinds of trusts," Lucas was saying, "and one of them is to protect money earned by somebody who's younger than eighteen or twenty-one or whatever, whenever it is that you get to be an adult. Like child movie stars. The money goes into a trust, so it legally belongs to the kid instead of the parent."

Keeping my voice as low as Lucas's, I said, "So you're saying all the money Seneca earns might go into a trust that would belong only to her, and not to her mom—"

"Or her stepdad. Money that's kept in trust is handled by somebody else. Like a bank or a law firm. But I think I read—meep, I wish I were more sure of this—that sometimes the parents can be the trustees. Anyway, I'm thinking the trustees, whoever they are, whether it's Teresa or some attorneys or whatever, would fork over big time if it was for a kidnapping ransom. Plus, for that huge amount they asked for—that's like a million bucks, you know—they could probably borrow money on the performing fees she would make in the future. I think only the most famous concert performers, like the ones who have been around for a very long time, would be rich enough to pay a one-million-dollar ransom."

Just then the kitchen door swung open, and a young man headed toward our table with two plates of food. The guy was tall like Jamie. He was the same age as Jamie. He had curly hair like Jamie. Big blue eyes with long lashes like Jamie. In fact, he looked a lot like Jamie.

"You're not Jamie," I said.

"You found me out," he said, setting our plates in front of us.

Now I was the one to blush. What a totally stupid thing to say, telling him he wasn't Jamie! I about wanted to die.

"I'm sorry," I said. "I mean—"

"Nae problem. I'm Robbie Wilson, Jamie's twin." His smile was even bigger than his brother's, and his eyes had a twinkle I hadn't noticed in Jamie's that made him look like he was happy, and laughed a lot. He made me feel . . . funny.

His hair was darker than his twin's. He saw me noticing, and I quick looked down at my plate.

"Can I get you lassies any coffee or tea?"

We shook our heads.

"Do you have a mum or dad comin' down to breakfast?"

Lucas said, "Her mom is coming, but she's not here yet. We're expecting her today."

Yeah, right.

Robbie was quiet for a second. I managed to look at him, and because of his expression, I expected him to ask how we got to Portree without parents. But his face changed, and instead he said, "Oh, aye. Well, is there anything else I can get for you lassies?"

I shook my head, and Lucas said, "Not for me."

"Enjoy your breakfasts, then." Smile smile, twinkle twinkle.

Lucas thanked him, I muttered out a thank you, and off he went.

"He's gorgeous," I whispered.

"What? No! Jamie's cuter!"

Lucas and I stared at each other. Finally she said, "They're too old for us. But they're so cute! Their eyes are amazing!"

"I love the way they talk, with that accent, and the little lilt in their voices. And I love their names, Jamie and Robbie."

It hit me that I probably shouldn't be spending time crushing on a guy, with Seneca held hostage in a castle outside of town. Lucas must have been thinking the same thing, because she said, "I'll bet they could tell us how to get to Old Dalhousie Castle. Or at least they'd know who to ask."

Lucas and I had talked about it the night before. We'd decided to make a daylight trip out to the castle to see where it was, see if we could figure out where Seneca could be, who else was around, all that kind of thing. Once we had it all scoped out, we'd decide what to do next to rescue her, but finding the castle was step one. "If we end up asking Robbie about it, would you mind doing the talking?" I asked.

"You do the same if it's Jamie."

Between the whole Robbie thing and our worries about Seneca and Parker, I thought I wouldn't be very hungry. But with the train rides the day before, we hadn't had even one good meal, and thirty seconds after our food got to the table, I was chowing down. I even ate the haggis, which looked and tasted kind of like a pile of ground beef, only with a liver flavor so tiny that I didn't mind it, and I hate liver. Like places we'd been in England and at the hotel in Edinburgh, each plate came with a little half tomato that had been fried or something—they call them *grilled to-mah-toes*—and fried mushrooms.

I ate everything except the tomato, and lined the silverware up on my big plate to show I was finished with it. I'd just put marmalade on my third half slice of toast and picked it up from my bread plate when Jamie, who had been pouring coffee for some other guests, turned to ask us how we were doing. I said we were doing fine, and just then Robbie came out of the kitchen.

"How was it?" Robbie asked, taking our plates.

I was saved from having to answer because my mouth was full of toast, and Lucas said, "It was good."

"Did you like the haggis, then?" Jamie asked.

We both nodded. I managed to swallow and said, "Yeah. What's in it that tastes like liver?"

"There is a little sheep's liver," Jamie said. "Along with some other parts of the sheep's insides."

We must have looked horrified, because Robbie said quickly, "And other things. Oatmeal, onions, suet, and spices."

Seneca or no Seneca, when I looked at Robbie I got that funny, fluttery feeling again. But Lucas was even worse. With Jamie around, her expression got all glazed over, and I decided that if one of us was going to ask about the castle, it was going to have to be me. Honestly, I was beginning to think that Lucas had lost almost all of her backbone to boys.

I took a deep breath, looked directly at Jamie, and said, "How would we get to Old Dalhousie Castle?"

"The best way is to hike there. There's a bit of a lane the construction people are using that leads to the castle from the main highway, but there are no buses that go anywhere near. It's two and a half miles up the coast. Is that where you want to go this morning?"

I nodded. It was impossible not to see Robbie out of

the corner of my eye, and my heart was beating like crazy. "How do we—" I broke off. My voice had sounded squeaky, so I focused and started over. "Where do we find the path?"

"It's not far from here, just at the end of the lane," Jamie said, pointing at the street the hotel was on. "Go left at the turning, and you'll see the path off to the right."

"It's lovely at the castle," Robbie said, with that lilting accent. It was odd to hear a boy call something *lovely*. I didn't think I'd ever heard an American boy using that word, and it made my heart go flip-flop even more. "They're doing work on it, restoring it. It will be a fine place when they're finished. You're lucky you chose a Sunday. When the construction is going on, they don't let tourists get near. But today with no workmen, you'll have it to yourselves."

Lucas and I looked at each other. "There will be workmen there tomorrow?" she asked.

"Yes, but today there would be just the tourists," he answered. "And not many of them. This late in the season, you'll be mostly alone there.

"We're expecting heavy weather in the night," he continued. "Rain and gale force winds all over the west of Scotland. But just now it looks like a grand mornin' for a wee walk."

A grand mornin' for a wee walk. My heart absolutely

turned upside down, even though walking two and a half miles one way and two and a half miles back didn't seem very wee to me. I wondered if Robbie would consider dating a younger woman.

Just then a couple came into the breakfast room. "Excuse me," Jamie said, and moved to greet them.

"Don't fail to take your rain gear if you're going to hike," Robbie continued. "The weather is always changing on Skye. We have the sunshine and the rain and the wind and the mist, and sometimes all of it at once. And whatever it is one minute, it'll be different the next."

Lucas and I looked at each other. We hadn't brought any rain gear. But she didn't say anything, and I was glad she didn't because I was afraid Robbie would think we were total idiots.

As soon as he left the table, Lucas whispered, "If they're going to have a construction crew out there tomorrow, it doesn't seem very likely that they're holding Seneca there. If they are, they must be going to move her to another place either today or early tomorrow morning!"

I'd been so busy thinking about Robbie that it took a minute for this to sink in. "You mean, so that there wouldn't be a whole bunch of workers around there who might see her."

"Exactly."

"Great! As if we didn't have enough problems, now

we have to worry about rescuing Seneca before she gets moved somewhere else!"

"Assuming she's there at all." Lucas sounded very discouraged. I still had the feeling that Seneca was at the castle—not just because of the "dollhouse castle in the sky" business and my intuition, but also because Paul had made that phone call to Portree—but the thought that we might have only a few hours or, at most, one day to rescue her made me feel just as discouraged as Lucas sounded.

"At least this storm isn't coming in until night," she said. "That's something anyway." She sighed. I was usually the one who sighed. Things must be pretty bad if Lucas was doing it.

"Let's just take things one step at a time," I said. "The first thing to do is to get some rain gear and get out to look at the castle. What do you think our chances are of finding a place open where we can get rain gear in Portree on a Sunday morning?"

"Not great," Lucas muttered back, as we left the breakfast room. "Let's ask the person at the front desk."

The person at the front desk turned out to be a woman with a name tag that said MRS. MACLEOD, who had straight brown hair and glasses. When Lucas asked her question about the rain gear, Mrs. MacLeod almost scowled, muttered that there was an outdoor shop just down the block that opened at nine on Sundays during tourist season, then said, "Are you the pair from room twelve who checked in without an adult?" Her voice was sour. Distinctly sour.

I saw a look in Lucas's eyes that made me wonder if she was going to come out with something like, "Yeah, you got a problem with that?"

So I quickly said, "Yes, my mother is expected today."

"How did you come to be here without her?"

"Um," I started, wondering why we hadn't taken the time to come up with a really good story about this.

But Lucas, of course, was ready with an answer. "Kari and I were staying with some friends of the family in Inverness while Kari's mother attended a conference in Glasgow. Kari's mother was supposed to meet us in Lochalsh last night, so the friends put us on the train. But while we were traveling, Kari got a text message saying her mom was delayed at her conference, and we should catch the bus and come up to Portree where we had hotel reservations. Kari and I are used to international travel, so it's not that big of a deal for us."

Mrs. MacLeod scowled, clicked her tongue as if she thought I must have a really terrible mother, and said, "Well, I hope she arrives soon. This is all very irregular."

"This is all we need!" I said as we headed for the outdoor store.

"Figure it this way," Lucas said, "Mrs. MacLeod is the least of our problems."

She had a point.

By nine thirty, Lucas and I had new anoraks in our backpacks along with some snacks and bottled water, Lucas's digital camera, and the opera glasses, which I was proud that I'd remembered to pack. Then, at last, we were out in the sunshine, on our way to the dollhouse castle in the sky.

24
Castle in the Mist

The harbor looked almost as beautiful in the morning light as it had the night before. Clouds were speeding around up above, so once in a while the sun got blocked off, but a minute later it would shine again, and when it did, the colors of the shops looked especially bright. The blue-gray water was busy with boats, and they were colorful, too—brightly painted sailboats and rowboats, and green and blue fishing boats with red or orange tops. There were seagulls flying and shrieking overhead.

"What are those big red things on the boats that look like beach balls?" Lucas asked.

"Floats, I think. Maybe to hold their fishnets and mark where they've left them." It always feels so weird when Lucas asks *me* about things she doesn't know, instead of the other way around. But when it comes to boats and most other things that have to do with water, I'm the expert, because I've been staying a lot with my dad on his houseboat since I was three. And it's not enough that he lives on a boat. When he and I go away for weekends, we almost always go to Lake Superior and hang out around the boats and the big ships. A few times we've even rented a sailboat. My dad is definitely a boat kind of guy.

We found the path, no problem, and soon we were walking above the coastline, with the Portree harbor behind us. Across the water was another island with patches of heather and high, misty hills. The steep field to our left was covered with knee-high heather and lots of some kind of evergreen bushes. A few sheep with long, black ears and faces were scattered here and there looking down on us.

This made me think about Mom, because it was the kind of scenery she'd go all nuts over. I liked it, too. In fact, if I'd been in a better mood I'd have probably wanted to paint it. I'm pretty good at painting, and I like to do it. But there was way too much bothering me, and it wasn't just Seneca and Parker.

"Lucas," I said. "I've been thinking about Jamie and Robbie."

"Me, too. Don't you think Jamie looks reckless, like the hero in an action flick?"

"I'm not sure about the hero business, but he does have a little bit of reckless in him. I can see that. But you can tell Robbie has a great sense of humor. And he's smart and kind."

"Jamie looks smart, too," she said, like she was defending him.

"Lucas—"

"Yeah."

"I'm not sure we should be thinking about this with Seneca in the castle and everything. Besides, have you thought about that gorgeous blond desk clerk who was there when we came in last night? She's about their age."

"Meaning . . . Oh, I get it. Oh, meep."

"What do you bet they're both interested in her?"

"You're probably right." We crunched along on the gravel for a while. "Okay, I'm not stupid enough to try to compete. But just because they're too old for us and probably have the hots for somebody else doesn't stop me from thinking Jamie is seriously cute."

Somehow I didn't even have the energy to say that Robbie was cuter, or to ask anything about Mr. Makes Me Want to Gag.

Having to give up my fluttery feeling about Robbie left me with nothing to think about but Seneca and Parker, and *that* left me feeling depressed and worried and nervous, just like I'd been pretty much constantly since the kidnapping.

The path was broad enough for us to stay side by side. We walked fast, sometimes trotting.

Once, when we'd been running and we were out of

breath, I said, "It sucks that we'll have to make this whole trip to the castle again."

"That's assuming Seneca is actually there and we figure out how to rescue her. It'll be worse if we *don't* have to come out again because she's not there or we can't figure out a way to get her out of there."

I had my private thought about the dungeon again. "If Seneca's there, I'll bet they'll have a guard there."

"I wondered about that, too."

"At least we'd be pretty sure that Seneca was there, and that would be good. Well, not just good. It would be, like, wonderful. But if there's a guard, and he sees us and chases us off, we'll have to come back a second time to do our scouting."

"That's if all he does is chase us off."

I let that sink in for a minute.

Pretty soon we rounded a bend and saw an enormous bluff in the distance. The sky above it looked almost lavender. Reflecting it, the water was practically purple. And of course there was all that purple heather. It was just like the picture we'd seen in the brochure. I hoped that Seneca wasn't in a dungeon and instead was in a part of the castle where she could look out on the nice morning.

But just like Robbie had predicted, the weather didn't stay nice for long. Slowly the mist that had been hanging around the hills on the island across that little bit of sea dipped down and headed our way. The sun disappeared behind a thick layer of gray clouds, making it suddenly a lot darker and cooler. We stopped and put on our jackets. At this point the trail was just wide enough for one. We hoisted our backpacks and set out again, Lucas leading the way.

The mist spread slowly in our direction, wispy at the front, more solid behind. It seemed like the place just couldn't stop being purple—even the mist was lavender-gray. The island we'd seen earlier was invisible now. Nearer to us, where the air was still clear, the sea was black as a crow.

Below the big bluff I'd seen from the distance, the path was high up above the sea and curved slowly to the left. As we came around the bend, we felt a cold, damp breeze coming off the water. I zipped up my jacket. Lucas put her hood up, and a minute later, so did I.

We'd been curving left a long time when all of a sudden Lucas stopped, stepped backward (just missing my toe), grabbed the bottom of my jacket, and pulled me to the ground with her.

In the split second before I went down, I saw at least part of what she'd seen: Old Dalhousie Castle on the little point of land sticking out into the sea, the castle and its surrounding wall almost as black as the water around them.

"There's somebody down there," she said.

I got up on my hands and knees, level with the bushes

beside the path. Below us, the harsh and cheerless castle itself and the surrounding wall with its cutout battlements were nothing but dark shapes against the lavender-gray of the distant mist.

"Not toward the front," Lucas said. "Look on the side, about halfway along, before where the outside wall starts to crumble."

I could see both the front of the wall with its big gate and the whole side that led almost to the water before it became just a big pile of ruins. Sure enough, halfway along I saw a guy—actually, I saw a light-colored shape against the dark background and just figured it must be a guy. I didn't know how Lucas had managed to spot him so quickly.

Lucas scooted up beside me, looking through the opera glasses. "*He* has binoculars. He's just putting them up."

"Can I have a look?"

She put out her hand as if to shut me up, then said, "Get down, he's looking at the path." This time, instead of pulling me, she pressed on my shoulder.

We lay flat, heads on the ground, invisible because of the height and curve of the trail and the plants that grew beside it. I don't know how long we lay that way—long enough for the bumps of the gravel to feel uncomfortable. This could get scary, I thought, but having a guard there was just what we'd been hoping for.

At last we crept forward on our stomachs until we

could see it from ground level. A few yards up ahead was
a sign:

DALHOUSIE CASTLE IS UNDERGOING RENOVATION.
PLEASE DO NOT PASS BEYOND THIS POINT
MONDAY THROUGH FRIDAY,
0800 THROUGH 1800
PASSAGE BEYOND THE CASTLE'S OUTER WALLS
IS STRICTLY FORBIDDEN AT ALL TIMES.

Underneath, it said what we figured was exactly the
same thing in Gaelic.

Lucas handed me the opera glasses. "It's your turn to
look."

"His binoculars are down," I said. "If we go much farther on the path, he's going to be able to see us even when
we're on the ground."

"Let's hide in the heather and the bushes," Lucas said,
saying what I was thinking.

I took a deep breath. "If we're going to do it, let's go
now."

We scrambled a few yards down the hill, where the
bushes were thicker. And not a moment too soon. I looked
through the opera glasses again, peering through a gap
in the prickly, needle-covered branches. The man lifted
his binoculars and seemed to aim them directly at us. My
heart jumped so much that it hurt, and I ducked back.

"Stay down," I hissed. After that first rush of fear, my heart was pumping hard and fast, the sound whooshing through my ears.

I took a deep breath and tried to get calm. As scared as I felt, I knew in my mind that the man couldn't see me. It wasn't just that there was a bush between us. We'd bought gray-and-black jackets especially so we'd blend in. On this gloomy day, with our hoods up and our dark blue jeans, we were about as well camouflaged as we could get.

That didn't stop me from being afraid. I raised my head to the little peek hole in the bush and was about to look through the glasses again when a gull screamed directly overhead. I jumped and grabbed for Lucas's arm.

"It's just a bird," she said. She sounded calm, as usual, but she didn't have the impatient sound in her voice that she sometimes has when I get scared and she doesn't. Like I said, she's almost never afraid—about the only thing she's scared of is spiders—but she seemed to understand why I was freaking.

I calmed myself down a second time, raised the glasses, and managed to get a good, long look at the guy standing guard.

"Lucas, I think it's Green Socks!" I handed her the opera glasses. "I just noticed the color of his jacket."

"You're right! It's bright green! What do you bet it's a Celtic jacket? And he has a shaved head. That has to be him!" She turned to me, her eyes full of excitement. "That means Seneca's actually in there!"

"I knew it! I just knew it!" I had known it, I guess, but that didn't stop me from feeling huge relief.

Lucas looked through the opera glasses again. "Okay, his binoculars are down. Let's get closer!" And with that she started forward, on her feet but bent over at the hips to stay low to the ground, with me right behind her.

He kept on with the same routine—lifting his binoculars every minute or so, looking at the path, then dropping them. He even did it when he was smoking a cigarette, which was a lot of the time. We kept up our routine, too, moving from one clump of bushes to another.

While this was going on, I had a lot of time to look at the castle. I'd probably only seen the picture Jock had shown us for half a minute or so, and that photo had been taken from way up the hill. But the castle looked like it had in the brochure: a tallish, dark, grim building surrounded by a wall with battlements, all of it built on a point that stuck out into the sea.

Now I looked at the details. The castle itself wasn't all that big. It was hard to tell exactly—you could only see the part of the building that stuck up over that wall—but I figured it was five or maybe six stories high, with a pointed roof that was falling in at the back, and as I'd noticed on the tourist brochure, the building was taller than it was wide and had only slits for windows. There were round turrets on each corner, but otherwise the castle walls were flat.

The wall that surrounded it, like a very tall and super-thick stone fence, made the whole place look bigger. It was probably two stories high, with the battlement cutouts marching all the way around the top of it. A few of the wide stone teethlike things had lost their corners, but most were in pretty good shape. I figured the wall had been built to be the outside of a moat, back when they had moats. There was a wide entrance on the side farthest from the sea, where the gate must once have been. But there was no gate there now, just an empty space with a white van parked in front—the van Seneca must have been taken away in. When the castle was built, the side of the battlement wall nearest us probably went all the way out into the water, but now the part close to the shore had crumbled completely into just a pile of rocks.

The only way this castle would be in a book of fairy tales was if it was the place where the evil witches were holding the princess.

The closer we got, the more worried I was that we'd be spotted. We were near enough to see what the guy was doing without using our opera glasses, when suddenly he looked up in our direction while we were moving from bush to bush. We dropped into the heather and stayed that way. My heart was pumping loud in my ears. We'd been caught. He'd come for us. Should we wait, or should we start running now?

But the silence stretched out, and nothing happened. Finally Lucas, who had the opera glasses, lifted them to her eyes and peeked up over the plants.

"It's okay. He's lighting another cigarette."

I heaved a big breath of relief.

When we got to the last big clump of bushes, about as far away from Green Socks as the length of the soccer field at my school, Lucas said, "Let's stay here for a while and look."

The castle loomed up in front of us, nearly black, all bleak and cold-looking. The outer wall with its battlements blocked off our view up to the second story, but we could see three floors sticking up above that. Lucas had her camera out and was using her zoom lens to take pictures of everything.

That was fine with me. I didn't want to go any farther. Besides, now that we were pretty sure that Seneca was actually there—at least if having a guard was a clue—it was a good place for trying to spot exactly where they might have put her. Assuming she wasn't in a dungeon.

The sea, which had been only one of a bunch of sounds when we were up on the path, was incredibly noisy here. The waves roared on the rocks, almost drowning out the screams of the gulls. The mist was just reaching land. The first wisps of it had settled around one side of the main building and down over one section of the battlements, like fingers of a giant ghost slowly closing over the black stones. I shivered.

I don't know exactly when I focused on the birds. I think I was just sort of staring at them without seeing them, thinking about how eerie everything was, when suddenly they came into focus: gulls, dozens of them, swooping down to one place behind the outer wall and screeching, then circling above and swooping and screeching again.

"Lucas, look at those gulls. What are they doing?"

I lifted the opera glasses to look at the birds, and Lucas did the same, using her camera.

"Someone's throwing food out for them," she said. Then, with a little gasp, she said, "Kari, I think it's Seneca!"

25
Hiding in a Moat

I tilted my glasses up, and there she was, just inside the little window slit on the third floor, steadily and with a kind of rhythm tearing up some kind of food—white, so probably bread—and tossing pieces of it out the window to the screaming gulls.

"I can't see her face very well, can you?" Lucas asked.

I watched through the opera glasses for a few seconds. "Not really," I answered. "I know it's her because of the color of the skin of her arms, but her face is just an outline because it's so shadowy up there."

Lucas was squinting through the viewfinder of her camera. "Yeah. I wish she'd step forward, or the sun would come out or something."

"She must not be freezing, or she wouldn't have the window open. I wonder if they gave her warm clothes."

"I wish we could get her attention. How can we get her to look at us?"

"Without Green Socks seeing us, you mean? I don't think. . ."

But Lucas was already hitting a button on her camera that made her flash go off.

"Lucas," I hissed. "He'll see you for sure if you do that! Besides, from where she is, she can't tell there's anybody guarding her." Green Socks was right at the bottom on our side of the outer wall. "What if she sees us and yells?"

Lucas sighed. "I guess you're right. I wish we could talk to her and have her help us figure out how to rescue her! At least we've got to get into that moat. See if there's a way to get in through an entrance or a window. We'll have to go over that rock pile down there."

I looked to where she was pointing, where the wall, which must once have led into the sea, had totally crumbled. She was right—assuming Green Socks and Mustache wouldn't let us walk right into that huge gap where the front gate had once been, it was the only place where we could get inside the outer wall without any problem. Except for one thing.

"Um, and how are we going to do that without Green Socks noticing—" I broke off, feeling stupid. "Oh. The mist."

"Mm-hmm," Lucas said. "It's coming in our direction. And when it gets here, he won't be able to see us."

It was going to take a while. We waited and watched

as the mist settled in wisps and puffs over one part of the castle, then another.

I kept looking up at Seneca's window. For the first time, I noticed that the window slits like the one where she was standing weren't just holes in the wall. The castle wall was thick, but if you looked carefully you could see that all the slits actually had glass windows on the inside. I figured this was part of the renovation.

Seneca finally ran out of whatever she was feeding the gulls, and her window slowly swung closed.

This whole thing was a huge, huge relief to me. Seneca was alive, actually here at the dollhouse castle in the sky, just like we'd thought she'd be, and not in a dungeon. And in addition to being warm enough to have her window open, she must have enough to eat since she was throwing some kind of food to the gulls. Even though we hadn't rescued her, I felt happy.

We settled back in to wait for the mist. It seemed like getting to the castle had taken hours, but when I looked at my watch, it turned out to be five past eleven. We'd started only about an hour and a half before, and we'd walked two and a half miles, so we hadn't made bad time. We ate most of the trail mix we'd brought, sipped our water, and finished off with our Kit Kat bars. By the time we were done, it was half past. With the mist coming in, it was getting colder, but the mist still wasn't thick enough around us to hide in.

While we waited, I spent a lot of time looking at Green Socks through the opera glasses. He was probably in his twenties, with a thin face, eyes too close together, and ears that stuck out too far. He wore an earring in one ear. When he reached inside his jacket for a cigarette, which he did every five minutes or so, I could see a necklace with a big cross on it at the V-neck of his shirt. It made me think of the Celtics having mostly Catholic fans. He mainly spent his time walking back and forth, and a couple times I saw him hunch his shoulders as if he was cold.

Once he reached down and fiddled with the front of his pants. It took me a second to figure out what he was up to, then I said, "Oh, ick, he's going to the bathroom!" And Lucas and I turned our heads away for a long time, wrinkling our noses because the thought was so disgusting, until we were absolutely sure he was done.

By this time, the tiny drops of mist were all around us. Our jeans, already soaked at the knees from the wet grass and leaves, became wet all over, and freezing cold. My bangs stuck to my forehead. I felt the cold dampness climb in under my jacket, under my hood, and around the back of my neck.

Green Socks, just barely visible now, seemed to feel it, too. He stopped looking through the binoculars—there was no way to see the path—and sped up his walking, stomping as he went. Cigarette in his right hand, he hugged himself with the other, cradling his left hand under his right arm.

At last I saw him say something—I figured he was

swearing to himself—then he threw down his half-smoked cigarette, turned, and stomped off around the corner of the wall to the entrance side.

I would have stayed where we were to see if he'd come back, or maybe waited for the mist to get a little thicker, but Lucas said, "Into the moat we go," and off she went, me following behind her, the two of us running, keeping down and close to the ground like we had before.

We ran, walked, and stumbled our way through heather and brush, over stones and through a few puddles, to the part of the outer wall closest to the shore. From what I'd seen in that History Channel show where they talked about medieval castles, I figured that whoever had built it had had the bright idea to make it both the wall around the moat and a place soldiers could use to fight anybody who was trying to attack the castle. The top of the wall was flat and probably four or five feet wide, so the men could stand on it while they were shooting arrows or throwing boiling oil or whatever. The broad parts that were like teeth were about as high as my shoulders, and the spaces between them would come up to my knees.

The pile of rocks where the wall had crumbled was wide but not very high. Stepping our way over was a lot like trying to cross a rocky stream. We'd balance first on this steady rock, then test around us before we found the next one we could put our weight on. Once a rock I tried to step on rolled away with a clatter.

My heart started knocking and, cold as I'd been the

second before, I felt hot and sweaty. "Let's go back!" I said.

"Don't be silly, Kari. That sound would be totally drowned out by the waves and the gulls."

I wasn't so sure about the sound. I was getting more and more nervous with every passing second. But Lucas kept on going, so I followed.

At last we were over the rock pile. I didn't realize I wasn't breathing until all the air came out of my lungs in one big breath.

The space between the wall and the castle was maybe twenty feet wide. On the inside of the wall you could still see the line where the water from the moat had once been. Now the space was filled up with weeds and shrubs and little trees. Ahead of us, the plants seemed to have been mowed or pulled out—we couldn't quite see in the mist—by the people doing the renovations. But where we were, we had to walk through tall thistles covered with huge thorns, with big blooms at the top—lavender, of course—and shrubs with sharp branches. I was glad we had jeans on, even if they were wet and, now, very cold. At least they kept us from getting all scratched up.

All the way along, my heart was beating fast and my mouth felt dry. I turned constantly, looking behind us, then forward, sure somebody would come around the corner and we'd be taken prisoner like Seneca. Or worse.

Lucas, fearless as ever, snapped pictures as fast as she could.

We were almost under the window where we'd seen Seneca when I caught a whiff of cigarette smoke. I grabbed Lucas, and the two of us fell together into the weeds and bushes next to the wall, my right cheek smack down on a thistle plant.

Lucas let out a big "Ugh," and I gave a yell as the thistles went into my face. I lay completely tense, hoping the sounds were covered by the cries of the gulls, my heart thudding for the billionth time that morning, tears pouring out of my eyes from the pain.

The roar of the sea was more muffled here between the outer wall and the castle, but with the crashing of the waves and the screeching of the birds, it was maybe half a minute before I heard anything from the person who was smoking. Finally there was the sound of footsteps moving through the brambles.

My heart was pounding hard, and the fear and the pain combined to make me want to throw up.

But I stayed flat, silent, not moving a muscle, staring at the back of Lucas's head.

The smell of smoke was stronger now, totally covering up the smell of the dirt, making me feel even sicker— cigarette smoke always makes me sick. He was so close I could actually see him step over a thistle plant. His shoes and, sure enough, green-and-white socks stopped not six feet away from us.

"Nothin' here," he shouted. His accent was thicker

than any I'd heard in Scotland so far. I almost didn't understand even those two words.

A voice came from some way behind him. "Go on. Fairther. I know I haird somethin'."

"You do it, then!" Green Socks yelled back. I couldn't understand what he shouted next, but it was something about "bramble patch" and "trousers." He threw down his cigarette, like he was mad. It landed in the space between Lucas and me, the lighted end less than an inch from Lucas's hood and three inches from my nose. I caught my breath, but once again the sound I made was drowned out by the cries of the gulls.

"You and your sodding football wear! I [swear word] can't wait until we're out of here tomorrow morning and I'm [swear word] rid of you."

"Don't start [something something] on me again, you old [something]."

The two men were yelling now. Green Socks, still only feet away from us, was probably swearing as much as Mustache, only I couldn't understand him.

I held my breath as long as I could, but sometime in the middle of this I had to take a gasp, and when I did, I was almost overwhelmed by the gross cigarette smoke. Now I was feeling *really* sick.

At last Green Socks walked away, and the shouting voices moved around the side of the castle.

"Stay down," I said as I grabbed the cigarette butt and

stubbed it out. I realized as I did it that I needed to stand up, stay still, and breathe some fresh air to get rid of the sick feeling in my stomach, but there was no way I was going to hang out in that moat for one more second than I absolutely had to. "Let's get out of here," I said, and got to my feet.

We were climbing back over the pile of rocks before I noticed the cut in Lucas's forehead above her right eyebrow. At the same moment I looked at her face, she looked at mine.

"Holy schmack, Kari," she said, her eyes wide. "What happened to your face?"

I couldn't answer. I leaned forward and threw up all over the rocks.

26
Cheek Freak's Brilliant Idea

What I remember most about walking back to Portree was how totally miserable I felt. Being sick had left a horrible taste in my mouth, water didn't help, and my stomach didn't feel well enough for me to eat something to make the taste go away. The legs of my pants were soaking wet from the mist, my thighs were like ice, and I was freezing all over.

But mostly I was miserable because of the pain from the thistles. It felt like I'd had about a hundred vaccinations in my cheek all at the same time.

When we were far enough from the castle that we couldn't see it through the mist, Lucas looked more closely at my face. I'd pulled six thorns out myself, and I could feel gouges from my temple all the way down to my jaw. I was probably incredibly lucky I hadn't gotten stuck in the eyeball. Two of the thorns had broken off and the ends of them were still in there, but Lucas got hold of them with her fingernails and pulled them out, which hurt like meep. Then she soaked some Kleenex with water and cleaned the dirt off, and that hurt almost as bad.

Whenever both her hands weren't busy helping me, she was holding a wadded-up Kleenex to the cut on her own forehead, which bled like crazy but she said didn't hurt much. When she finished with me, I cleaned off her cut. Actually it was more like a scratch. Even though it bled a lot, it didn't seem to be very deep.

We must have looked seriously lame trudging back, covered with mud from lying on the ground, each of us holding Kleenex up to our bloody faces. But at the time it didn't seem funny, and it sure wasn't fun. I couldn't believe plain old thistle thorns could hurt so bad. In fact, I probably shouldn't admit this, but part of the time I actually cried. I've practically never cried because something hurt me since I was in, like, first grade. I think it was the combination of pain, cold, wet, and that awful taste of vomit still in my mouth that pushed me over the edge.

We hardly said anything on the walk, just concentrated on putting one foot in front of the other. About halfway back, Lucas said something about what Mustache had said about leaving the castle the next morning, and about how we had to come up with a plan to rescue Seneca before they took her somewhere else.

I said, "Not now, Lucas. I feel like meep." And then

we were quiet again, and the only sounds were a bird chirp-
ing here and there, a sheep bleating, the murmur of the
sea—sometimes closer, sometimes farther as we followed
the path—and the *crunch crunch* of the gravel as we plod-
ded along.

The mist that had come in so thick and so slowly went
out in a rush. I thought Minnesota weather changed fast,
but ours doesn't even come close to the weather changes
on Skye. It was like the mist was there one minute, and
five minutes later it had moved out onto the sea. It left a
rainbow between it and us, one of those full, really bright
and beautiful rainbows that go all the way from one side of
the sky to the other.

A rainbow is supposed to mean a happy ending. At
that moment, it didn't feel like one was possible.

I know it doesn't seem like much compared to everything
that was going on with Seneca, but even though I was
trying to give up my thing for Robbie, when we got back
into town I was thinking about how I was going to get to
our hotel room without having him see me with my bloody
cheek. As it turned out, that wasn't a problem. When we
got to the lobby, Mrs. MacLeod was standing in the doorway to an office behind the desk area talking to someone,
her back to us. I was afraid she was going to turn around
and say something to us about Mom not showing up yet,
but we made sure we walked on the carpet the whole way

so she wouldn't hear our footsteps, and we managed to get around the corner to the staircase without her noticing us.

The only pants we had were the jeans we were wearing—I hadn't packed any extras—and our heaviest tops besides our hoodies were long-sleeved T-shirts. So Lucas washed her face carefully so her scratch wouldn't start bleeding again, combed her hair in a way that covered almost the whole thing, and wiped as much of the mud off her jacket as she could. Then she went out shopping.

I was already feeling a little bit better and a whole lot warmer by the time she got back, because I'd found some ibuprofen in the bottom of my backpack and it was working, I'd brushed my teeth, made myself a cup of tea with the tea-making things in our room, eaten one of the two packages of shortbread cookies they always left next to the teapot, and taken a shower.

Seeing myself in the mirror was a shock. My right cheek looked at least as bad as it felt, and that was saying a ton. It was bright red and stuck out—I thought I looked like a one-sided chipmunk with the measles—so I wrapped some ice from our little refrigerator in a washcloth and held that on it for about fifteen minutes. That seemed to help with both the pain and the swelling, but when I looked at my reflection again, I still thought of myself as the Cheek Freak. I would have laughed if it hadn't hurt so much.

The errands only took Lucas about forty minutes—

Portree is a very small town—and it would have been even quicker if she hadn't stopped to make sure there were still no e-mail messages from our moms. She'd bought new jeans for both of us, heavy wool sweaters, wool socks, some makeup for my face, plus two tubes of stuff to put on my thorn punctures and scratches. One of them really helped take the pain away.

Lucas took her shower while I tried on some makeup. It stung like crazy when I was putting it over the scratches and holes, but it made me look less like something out of a horror movie and more like I had a bad case of acne that strangely affected only one side of my face. We turned the radiator on low and let our dampish anoraks dry over it and our shoes dry under it while we got ready. Then we dressed in our new dry jeans and warm sweaters and socks. It's amazing what a dry, clean, warm set of clothes can do for you when you've been trekking around the countryside in cold, wet ones.

The twins weren't in the lobby. I was glad about that, even if I was looking better than I had when we came in.

I thought there might be some information about the castle in the tourist office, which we'd passed walking from the bus stop the night before. Sure enough, they had a brochure with a picture of the castle on the front of it. It had a map showing the walking path, but I noticed that there wasn't anything about the track that Green Socks and Mustache must have used to get their van to the castle. The brochure had a lot about the history of the place—mostly about fighting between families and massacres and things—and just what we were looking for: a floor plan. Somebody had put a sticker on the back saying almost exactly the same thing we'd seen on the sign near the castle—both the English and Gaelic versions.

When we were done at the tourist office, we went down to a fish-and-chips shop that was in one of those colorful buildings along the harbor. It was almost two o'clock, and we were both starved.

After spending the whole morning outside, I'd rather have sat in some nice, comfy restaurant, but the Cheek Freak in me wanted to keep away from people who might stare, and it was nice enough weather now, with sunshine only sometimes covered up with clouds.

Lucas stood in line at the window. I suddenly felt bad that I'd questioned her backbone earlier. In the past few hours she had really taken care of us, just like the "normal" Lucas would have done. I guess boys were her only weakness. Now that I'd met Robbie, I was beginning to wonder if they were becoming mine, too. But that thought was for another time.

While I waited for Lucas, I watched what was happening in the harbor. The boats were zipping in and out. A sign advertised boat tours for viewing sea eagles. If things hadn't been so weird, I would have loved to do that.

I also watched the gulls diving at the people trying to eat what they'd bought in the shop. Once I heard a woman let out a little scream, and when I looked over, I saw a gull fly away with a chunk of the woman's fish dangling from its beak.

So when Lucas came back with our little paper platters of steaming hot fish-and-chips, two Cokes under her arm, we took all of it up to the top of the stairs and had our picnic sitting on a low stone wall, away from the gulls.

"Lucas," I said, squeezing some mayo out of a little packet to use for dipping.

"Yes?"

"Um, I've been wondering. Now that we know where Seneca is and everything, do you think we might be able to report her kidnapping to the police?"

Lucas, who had just taken a bite of fish, looked out at the view, thinking about this.

"I mean, we have pictures of her in the castle. That would be pretty good proof. Why don't we just go and tell them the story and let *them* rescue her?"

"There are still problems with that, Kari. First, look at these pictures of Seneca." Lucas wiped her hands on her napkin, got her camera out of her backpack, and sorted through the photos she'd taken of the castle. "See? I didn't get a good picture of her. It was so dark, and the wall was so thick and the slit was so narrow. Plus her skin is dark, so she blended into the shadows."

She was right. We could see Seneca's arm and the birds and even the pieces of bread or whatever it was she'd been throwing out, but there was no way you could tell who it was.

"They might be able to make the pictures better in their police lab, though," I said. "You know, blow them up or do something with a computer or something so they could see the details."

Lucas thought about this for a minute. "I don't think anything is a whole lot different from the way it was when we were in Edinburgh talking about this," she said. "There's still the problem of us being kids, and of them probably calling Paul and Teresa right away the minute we got done telling our story.

"And if they didn't believe us—well, this is a pretty small town. What if the policeman or policewoman we talked to went out to have a beer after work and started talking about the crazy story these two fourteen-year-olds told them? And what if one of the other people at the pub was the person who gave Green Socks and Mustache the key to the castle or whatever? Then Seneca would be in even *more* danger."

"Yeah, I guess you're right." I sighed and stared out at the water for a while. "So do you have any ideas of how *we* can rescue her?" I asked.

She nodded, licked a dot of mayo off her finger, wiped the grease off her hands with a napkin again, and spread out the castle floor plan on the wall between us. "We get climbing equipment in the outdoor store, and after dark we go back into the moat and climb the castle wall up to Seneca's window. Like climbing a cliff face."

I just stared at her. "Lucas—" The only part of this plan I liked was waiting until dark.

"Look at this." She stared at the screen on the back of her camera, flicked through her photos until she found what she was looking for, and held it up for me to see. "The wall is so old that there are places where I could pound in the pitons you use in climbing. And there are those little windows, remember. And—"

This was taking the Lucas the Lionheart thing way too far.

"Lucas, hellooo." I waved a fry to get her attention. "You took exactly one single afternoon rock-climbing course at REI and you think you can climb a castle wall? You have got to be out of your meeping mind!"

"I could do it!"

"I'm sure you'd be brave enough to *try* it, but rock climbing up to a third-floor window on a building as old as that castle is something that amateurs shouldn't be messing around with."

"Why not?"

I couldn't believe that Lucas, as smart as she was, would say this. "Gravity, that's why not! Like, falling!"

"So do you have a better idea?"

I took the last bite of my first piece of fish, chewed, and swallowed before answering. "Not off the top of my head."

"See?"

"Lucas, don't hassle me. I'm not in the mood."

She took a deep breath and stuffed her mouth full of fries as if to keep herself from saying something she'd be sorry for. I wasn't feeling very friendly myself, probably because my cheek still hurt and I felt totally ugly, so I sipped my Coke and stared down at the harbor.

Lucas was the first one to talk. "I suppose you think we can just walk into the castle through, like, the front door or something."

I gave her a dirty look. "Of course not. Not with Green Socks and Mustache around."

"Did you see if the other guy *was* Mustache?"

"No, but I *suppose* it was. If it was somebody else, then maybe we have *three* guys keeping guard. Or *more*."

"Is there any way to get up on the roof?" Lucas asked. "Maybe we could go over the side to Seneca's window." She picked up the brochure. This time she held it up to look closely at the floor plan.

I thought the roof idea was almost as stupid as the wall climbing. Maybe even more stupid. I almost held my breath, worrying that she'd find an easy way to get onto the roof and I'd have to shoot her down again, pardon the pun, but it wasn't long before she sighed and set the brochure back down beside her.

"Well, if we can't do that, we're going to have to concentrate on figuring out how to get a rope into Seneca's room so she can tie it to something and lower herself on it."

"That's a great idea, Lucas!" I wanted to encourage her for saying something that wasn't completely insane for a change. "After it's dark, maybe we could get onto the part of the battlement where the soldiers would stand—what's that called?" They'd probably talked about this in that television show I'd seen, but I hadn't been paying enough attention to hear it, or at least to remember it. I knew Lucas would know.

"It's called a rampart."

So that's what they meant by *"O'er the ramparts we watched . . ."*

"The other part, with the crenellations, is the parapet," she added.

"The crenellations are the cutout parts that look like stone teeth?"

She nodded.

I used my last fry to scrape up the tiny bit of mayo I had left and popped it into my mouth. My lips barely moving because my mouth was full, I said, "If we stood on the rampart, it wouldn't be far to her window." I swallowed. "The problem is, how do we get her to open her window, and how do we throw the rope in?"

We were both quiet for a minute. Finally I said, "She'd probably open it if we threw teeny pebbles at the glass.

That's what they do in movies and things. But that doesn't solve the problem of getting the rope into her room."

"What if we punched a hole in a tennis ball and stuck the end of a rope inside it?"

I thought about that for a minute. "Wouldn't the rope drag the tennis ball down?"

"What if we got something really light, like thread? We could tie it to a ball and throw it across the moat, and she could pull on it, and we'd have the thread attached to a rope."

"Fishing line would be stronger than thread," I said.

And at that instant I had one of my most brilliant ideas ever.

"Lucas," I said, and grabbed her arm, "I know how to do this! I can *cast* the line over."

"Cast? What are you talking about?"

"Casting! Like fly-fishing casting! Like what my dad and I do together! What I won the contest in!"

Lucas was obviously not as excited about this as I was. "You mean like with a fishing pole?"

"With a fly rod, yes. I could put the line right inside her window."

"Seriously? You could do that?" She sounded very doubtful.

"Seriously! What we need to do is figure out how to make sure she knows she's supposed to pull. Like sending her a note somehow. Whatever it is, it has to be something really small and light. All we need is that, plus a rod and a reel and some fly line. And we might not even need the reel."

"You are actually saying you could stand up on that wall and cast a fishing line with a little note or something on it up into Seneca's window?"

"As long as the wind isn't too crazy, and the storm isn't supposed to hit until night. Even if it gets *pretty* windy, I know how to compensate for that. Unless there are forty-mile-an-hour crosswinds or something. At least I know I won't have a headwind because there'll be a huge castle in front of me."

"You're sure you can do this?"

I thought of the distance between the outer wall and Seneca's window, which was maybe twenty or twenty-five feet. Her window was higher than the top of the wall, but it wouldn't be any higher than the tip of my fly rod would be if I stood on the rampart and held it up. For the casting contest I'd won, I'd had two minutes to hit ten targets spaced between twenty and forty feet apart. I'd hit all ten using exactly twelve casts. I'd also hit targets using forehand and backhand casting, and I'd cast a line ninety whole feet. Maybe this all makes me sound like a total dork, but hey, what can I say? I rock at casting a fly line, and I'm not afraid to admit it.

"Lucas, I'm sure," I said. "I might have to try it a few times. It's overhead, and I've never cast to an overhead target before. But I can do this. Really I can. This isn't that hard."

She was staring at me.

I couldn't resist. I had to say it. "Sometimes it pays to be the Junior Casting Champion of Wabasha, Minnesota."

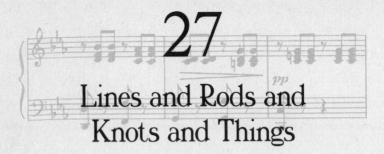

27

Lines and Rods and
Knots and Things

Like I said before, it felt odd knowing more about something than Lucas did.

We found out from the tourist office that the place to buy fishing equipment was the bicycle shop—who knew? Everything is only a couple blocks from anything else in downtown Portree, so our walk would have taken less than three minutes. But I made us stop and sit down on a bench on the small square in the middle of town.

"The first thing we have to do is figure out what kind of little thing we're going to have at the end of the line with the note on it telling Seneca to pull."

"Why?"

"Because then I'll know what weight fly line to get."

"It comes in different weights?"

I nodded. She looked at me like she thought I'd say more, but I was pretty sure she wouldn't be interested in hearing that the first thing you do to decide what weight line to use is to figure out what kind of bugs are eaten by the fish you want to catch.

We finally decided to use the smallest cork we could find or cut one down if we had to, and paste a tiny note on it with clear mailing tape. We'd punch a hole in the cork with a needle and string it with fly-tying thread. We'd get some climbing rope to attach to the fly line. When we were on the rampart across from Seneca's window, we'd attach a backpack to the rope, filled with some clothes and a jacket she could use for hiking—her hoodie plus the dress and high heels she'd been wearing for the concert probably wouldn't be the very *best* clothes for hiking two and a half miles, and who knew if there'd be time for her to change after we left the castle? Maybe we'd have to run because somebody would be chasing us.

With the clothes, we'd send a note telling her what to do: get into the new clothes, tie the rope to something close to the window that wouldn't move, then climb down the rope to the ground. Lucas would be waiting in the moat to show her how to get out.

Island Cycles was kind of strange, but fun. It was mostly bicycles for rent and for sale, and bicycle helmets and things. But there was fishing stuff on one side. It felt good to be looking at familiar things like feathers, colorful spools of tying thread, rods, and reels. But even knowing what I was looking at, I was nervous. Depending on the wind and how it would be to cast to an overhead target, having the right equipment could make the difference between easy and hard—and if the weather was bad enough, maybe the difference between being able to do it and *not* being able to do it.

I wished my dad was there to tell us about everything. I wasn't an expert, and I didn't want to ask the clerk what equipment I needed to cast a note on a cork from a battlement across a moat to an overhead window in the side of a castle.

Fortunately, the clerk was busy with somebody renting a bike who was asking a lot of questions, so I could wander around. The first thing I found was a package of five little cork floats perfect for what we needed. I took one out of the package, felt it in my hand, and tried to remember the lessons I'd learned from Dad over the years. I thought about what the weight of the cork plus note would mean to the cast, about air resistance if there was wind, about the length of the rod. I wondered about a reel. I didn't know if I needed one. Finally, right or wrong, I made a decision. (If you're interested, not that you would be, it was a nine-foot graphite fly rod and a weight-forward eight-grain line, and I decided not to get a reel.)

I let Lucas pick the color of the fly-tying thread. She decided on bright yellow. Then she paid for all this stuff with her credit card.

When we were done in Island Cycles, we had to do

the rest of our shopping. It meant going to a few places, but we finally got colored paper, clear mailing tape, a pair of scissors, a flashlight, and a thick needle. At a clothing store we picked out a wool sweater, jeans, socks, and undies for Seneca, guessing at sizes. Then we went to the outdoor store, where we got her a waterproof anorak—purple, which would blend into the Isle of Skye perfectly. Lucas picked out a hugely long length of climbing rope, plus we got waterproof rain pants for all three of us, and hiking boots for Seneca—we decided not to get hiking boots for the two of us, but at least one of us would have dry feet even if it rained. Fortunately we happened to know her shoe size because I'd once tried on her fancy concert heels. And Lucas remembered to get gloves, so Seneca wouldn't hurt her hands.

Last, we stopped by the grocery store and got some freezer bags with airtight seals, the strongest ones we could find.

As the stuff we bought mounted up and Lucas signed more and more credit card slips, I thought that if there was ever a good time for shopping with someone who was able to throw money around big-time, this was it.

It had started spitting down rain, and there was a cold, stiff breeze. I'd broken down the fly rod, which means I'd taken it apart at the middle. There wouldn't be any problem getting it into the hotel—if we wanted to buy a rod, that was our business—but we figured some grownup might think it was *their* business to stop us if it looked like we were leaving to go out fishing when it was getting dark. So the last thing we did before going back to our room was head down to the trail and hide the fly rod in the heather behind a rock.

By the time we got to the hotel, it was a quarter to four. This time the lobby was empty, and there was a RING FOR SERVICE sign on the desk.

We quick checked our e-mail—nothing—made it up to our room, threw our stuff on the floor, took off our coats, and flopped onto our beds. I felt both tired and not tired. My body was worn out from the hike this morning and I think partly from what had happened to my cheek, plus all the errands this afternoon. But I was totally wired. I couldn't have gone to sleep if somebody had paid me a million bucks.

It took a while for us to get everything sorted out and arranged. We worked together taping notes that said *Pull* on a few corks—we wanted to make sure we had backups if something happened to the first one. Lucas put knots in the first half or so of the climbing rope to help Seneca come down it, just like she'd learned in her climbing class; the rope was so long, we didn't need knots in all of it. While she did that, I strung the fly-tying thread through the corks with the needle and tied them so they'd be ready to attach to the fly line when the time came.

Lucas watched me. "That's cool that you know how to make all those different kinds of knots."

"I have to do this kind of thing every time we go fly-fishing."

"Well, I have another job for you. I'll bet you know what kind of knot to use to fasten one end of a rope to something solid, right?"

I nodded. I had to do that on my dad's houseboat all the time.

"While I'm finishing with this rope, how about you write the note to Seneca and draw a picture of that knot on it so she'll know how to tie it to something in her room."

So I wrote the note telling her to change her clothes, then tie the rope to something that wouldn't move and climb down it to where Lucas would be waiting. At the bottom I drew a picture of the knot she should use: a round turn and two half hitches, which sounds like more than one knot, but really isn't.

When we finished, we stuffed Seneca's clothes and gloves into one of our backpacks, topped off with a freezer bag containing the note I'd just written. Finally we put two bottles of water, our leftover trail mix from this morning (in case Seneca was hungry), the flashlight, the scissors, the corks with their little notes stuck on, the fishing line, and the climbing rope into the other backpack.

When that was done, we left the room, planning to wander around town until it was time to have an early dinner. We figured that when we finished eating, it would be close enough to dark to start for the castle. I was worried that Mrs. MacLeod was going to be at the desk and hassle us about Mom again.

But it didn't turn out that way. Guess who was behind the desk when we reached the lobby: Jamie and Robbie.

Terrific. Just terrific.

"Hello, lassies. How was your walk to the castle?" Jamie asked.

Even though it was Jamie asking and I should have probably answered instead of making Lucas do it, I didn't say anything. I wanted to be invisible. Eventually Lucas realized she was going to have to talk, and she came up with, "Very picturesque. The mist came in." Not bad, I thought.

Robbie looked at me. "What happened to your face?" It would have to be Robbie who noticed first.

"She tripped and fell in some brambles," Lucas said. Then quickly, as if to change the subject, "Has Kari's mother called or anything?"

"No, havenae haird a word," Jamie answered. He lowered his voice to just above a whisper. "Mrs. MacLeod's getting a bit worried about when your mum is coming in."

"She'll be here before bedtime," Lucas said, sounding as if she really believed what she was saying.

"I hope she gets here in the next hour or two," Robbie said in his soft little lilt. "The bad weather and heavy winds are comin' in early. It'll be blowin' up a gale before long. They say it's going to storm all night long and into the mornin'."

My heart dropped down to the bottom of my stomach, as I pictured my fly line blowing sideways in the wind. I burst out, "You said at breakfast the storm wasn't supposed to be here until tonight!" The minute it was out of my mouth, I realized I sounded like it was all his fault.

"Aye, but it's comin' in fast," Robbie said with a smile.

This was the second stupid thing I'd said to him. He would think I was a 100 percent total idiot. I thought for a minute what I could say to make it better, but I ended up just looking at the floor.

Lucas covered for me again. "What time do they say now it will hit Portree?"

"Between seven and eight."

Lucas said, "Well, we'll get going and have an early dinner then."

"Here in Scotland, a meal at this time of day is called *high tea*," Robbie said. It was just after five.

"You might want to try the caff," Jamie said. "On your right along the main street. You can't miss it. They'll do a nice tea for you there."

Lucas turned to me. "Oops, we'd better go back to our room. I just remembered that I left my credit card in my backpack."

We both knew that the credit card was actually in her pocket.

She waited until we were back in our room, then said, "If Seneca's going to be moved in the morning . . ."

"We have to get out to the castle before the storm," I finished.

Ten minutes later, wearing wool sweaters, anoraks, and rain pants, backpacks in place, we waved good-bye to Robbie and Jamie as we passed the front desk and left the hotel. And three minutes after that, the broken-down rod in my hand, our pockets filled with tiny stones from the path to throw at Seneca's window, we were on our way.

28
The Cashmere Curtain

The walk seemed to take forever. It had stopped raining—once or twice we even saw a little sun—but the breeze was colder than it had been before.

At our first glimpse of the NO TRESPASSING sign up ahead, we dropped to the ground and crawled around the last curve, in case there was a guard on duty. Lucas had the opera glasses. We'd left the camera at the hotel.

"It's Mustache this time," she said.

"How about Seneca's window?"

"No light on yet."

"Does Mustache have binoculars?" I asked.

"Uh-huh. Same old routine. Let's get down the hill away from the path."

We did exactly what we'd done in the morning, and even went to the same place we'd been before, behind a big bunch of bushes close enough to see Mustache without using the opera glasses, ready to move fast if he went away to do whatever. If we could just get on the rampart, we'd be fine, way over Mustache's head so he'd never see us.

Lucas's pictures had shown that it would be easy to get onto the rampart from the crumbled wall we'd climbed over that morning. But getting to the rock pile was the problem, since we had to do it in daylight instead of at night like we'd planned. It was a quarter past six—the sun was behind the hills, but from what we'd seen the night before, it wouldn't be twilight for a couple of hours, even with the mountains blocking the sunshine. There was no mist, nothing to keep us hidden from Mustache. We'd just have to wait and hope we got a break.

"How long do you think he's going to stay out there?" I asked.

Lucas just shrugged.

The wind kept getting worse. It was the kind that doesn't seem to be blowing in only one direction. A gust here, a gust there, and you can't really tell where it's coming from. When we got where we were going, we'd be standing way up high on the wall, and we knew it would be much stronger there than it was where we were down below.

Robbie had talked about strong winds both times he'd mentioned the storm moving in. I gazed at the pieces of fly rod in my hand. Thank goodness I'd told Lucas I couldn't cast if the wind was too terrible, so I wouldn't be totally humiliated if it blew so bad it completely meeped up my chances. But being humiliated wasn't the problem. Rescuing Seneca was the problem.

Waiting gave me time to notice how much my cheek was hurting—I'd forgotten to bring the ibuprofen or the cream that made it feel better. I told myself not to think about how exhausted I was, but my tiredness was getting to me. I was hungry because we hadn't eaten dinner, but we had to keep our little bit of trail mix in case Seneca needed it.

The clouds turned black, almost blocking out what daylight there was. Seneca's light came on. It was eerie, like maybe from a candle or a lantern. It looked like light from a window in a horror movie—the whole place looked like something from a horror movie—but at least Seneca was there. Or, I thought, feeling discouraged, at least *somebody* was there.

I was still looking up at Seneca's room when Lucas said, "Mustache's cell phone just rang." Sure enough. I couldn't see the phone, but we were close enough for me to see him holding his hand up to the side of his head.

Lucas raised the opera glasses. "He has a finger in his other ear."

No wonder, I thought. With the sound of the wind and the roar the sea made down there, he probably couldn't hear a thing.

He lowered his head and twisted around, as if trying to find a better place to listen. Then he moved toward the front of the castle and disappeared around the corner.

"Let's go!" we both said at the same time, and ran, still ducked down, from bush to bush to bush, toward the sea end of the wall.

We got to the rock pile, walked carefully to where the rocks became an actual crumbly wall, then climbed on our hands and knees up the broken parts to the rampart. This was hard for me, because I was carrying the two pieces of rod in one of my hands.

I stood up and was hit with a blast strong enough to make my anorak flap around my arms and waist. Strands of hair blew sideways onto my face from underneath my tightly tied hood.

But for the first time since my face had landed on the thistle, I smiled. Because now that I was on top of the wall, I could tell that when I cast the line, the wind would be at my back. If I had to have wind, that's exactly where I wanted it.

I looked down into the moat between us and the castle. It was scary up there, at least for me. The rampart was about as far off the ground as the upstairs duplex where I live. I don't like being up that high, especially with nothing between me and the drop below, even when the wind *isn't* strong enough to blow me over the edge. Lucas marched along the top of the wall to the spot across from Seneca's window. She wasn't bothered by the gusts at all. I went more slowly, hanging on to the wide stone teeth, and when I had to pass one of the low cutout parts between them, I made sure I always had hold of either the last tooth or the next one.

I'm so afraid of heights that I'd decided even before we knew it would be windy that I had to be tied to one of the crenellation teeth things while we were standing up there. If I could have done what I needed to do with the crenellation in front of me, it wouldn't have been so bad. But for the important part of my job, I'd be facing the drop-off into the moat instead.

So the first thing we did was cut a section of rope and use it to tie me in place—one loop around my waist, one loop around the nearest crenellation, and just enough rope between to allow me to move around but keep me from falling over the side. We didn't tie Lucas, because she'd need to be in the moat when Seneca came down, plus it would never occur to Nerves of Steel Stickney that she could possibly fall.

With the wind so strong, it was no surprise that Seneca's window was closed. The walls of the castle were thick, and the window was probably twenty feet away from us across the moat plus five feet higher than our heads. We couldn't tell if Seneca was looking out, but if she was, she probably couldn't see us. To make this plan work, we had to get her attention.

We set our backpacks down. I put my rod together while Lucas arranged the rope—the part that wasn't tying me to the wall—in a nice circle below where I was standing. I threaded the fly line through the guides, which are the little metal loops that hold the line to the rod.

Lucas fastened the backpack to the rope, then sat on her heels and watched me work.

I was knotting the cork with the note on it to the end of the line, when over the wind I thought I heard a man's voice. Lucas must have heard it, too, because her head jerked like mine did. Mustache had come around the side of the castle into the moat. Now out of the wind, he was *still* talking on his cell phone, leaning against the castle wall where he could see us just by looking up.

"Meep!" I whispered.

We scooted away from the edge and flattened ourselves on the rampart. I set the rod down, and Lucas pulled the backpacks toward us.

For what seemed like the millionth time that day, we waited. Sometimes we heard Mustache's voice over the sounds of the waves and the wind. Sometimes it would be quiet for a long time and Lucas would lean forward, peek over the edge, then lean back and say, "Still talking," or just make a face.

Finally, after one of her peeks over the side, she said, "He's gone around the corner, but he's still standing there leaning against the wall. I can see his shoulder and his arm."

Minutes passed. We were sheltered behind the stone tooth, but the wind had gotten stronger and colder. I began to shiver, and I was even hungrier than I'd been before.

I was thinking about food when Lucas leaned over and said into my ear, "Look out to sea."

Across the water, the space between the two islands seemed to be filled with something huge and dark, like an enormous gray cashmere curtain. Moving our way.

"The storm!" I whispered.

"We have to act fast, Mustache or no Mustache. We'll just have to hope he doesn't turn around and look up."

Hope? Pray, I thought.

"But Seneca can't come down the rope with him in the moat! If Mustache turns, he'll see both of you!"

We were quiet a minute. This time it was Lucas who came up with an absolutely awesome idea.

Three minutes later, she said, "You good?"

My heart was in my throat, but I managed to answer, "Good as I'll ever be."

Slowly we stood up. The wind was so strong it was like being hit in the back with something solid. Our sleeves and the sides of our jackets snapped around us. I'm absolutely sure I would have been blown off the wall if it hadn't been for the tight rope between my waist and the parapet, and Lucas actually grabbed on to a crenellation to keep her balance.

Now that I was standing up, I could see Mustache still leaning against the wall just around the corner of the castle.

We hadn't been able to come up with a better idea for

getting Seneca's attention than throwing pebbles at her window, even though we knew that if one of the guys was in her room when it happened, our plan would be shot and all three of us could be in real danger. Now, with Mustache standing just around the corner, the risk was even bigger. We'd hoped to be able to throw pebbles at Seneca's window in handfuls. Instead, we sorted through what we had in our pockets for the smallest ones. While I held my breath, Lucas, who was a way better pitcher than I was, threw the tiniest pebble toward Seneca's window. Missed. I shot a glance at Mustache, who didn't seem to have heard anything. Lucas tried four times more and missed every time. By then, I was so disappointed and scared that I practically felt like crying. Finally, on the sixth try, it looked like the stone made it into Seneca's window slit.

I looked down again to check on Mustache. He was still there, his arm crooked and his elbow sticking out, as if he still had his phone clamped to his ear.

For a few seconds we stared at Seneca's window. Nothing. Lucas threw another pebble, missed again, but the second one seemed to go in. This time, instead of waiting, she kept throwing, one after another—one in, two out, two in. I wanted to tell her not to—what if Green Socks was in Seneca's room? But I kept myself from saying anything. What else could we do?

"Please, let Green Socks not be there, and please,

Seneca, open the window!" I whispered. I looked out to
sea. The gray cashmere curtain was closing in. We didn't
have any time to spare.

What if she wasn't there? What if she'd been taken to
a different room and nobody was there at all? What if this
was the dining room or a living room or something, and
her bedroom was on the other side?

Just then I thought I saw the window move—or was it
only a flicker from a candle or lantern? Another pebble hit
the glass.

Suddenly the window swung open and Seneca's head
appeared, a shadow against the dim light behind her. She
looked straight out, then her head tilted down in our
direction.

As if we'd practiced it, which we hadn't, we both made
sh signs with one hand and frantically pointed down at
Mustache with the other. It looked like Seneca was trying
to get her head far enough out to look below into the moat
and see what we were pointing at, but she would have had
to turn her body sideways to get through the narrow slit.
She gave up.

I put my forefinger and thumb together in an *okay* sign
and, glancing to make sure Mustache hadn't come around
the corner, moved my arm around in the air to make sure
she saw it. Then I held my hand out flat like a traffic cop
and motioned for her to move back.

Suddenly I had this huge fear that she'd close her

window. Lucas must have thought the same thing, because she was making a cranking motion with one hand, pointing down at the movement with the other, and shaking her head so hard I thought she'd get dizzy. The next second we were hit with a fresh wind gust, and she had to stop and grab on to the rope that held me to the crenellation.

I settled into position. The cork was bobbing madly in the wind. The line it was tied to ran down the rod, through the metal guide closest to me, dipped to the ground and up again, where I held it loosely in my left hand. From there it led down to the neat circle of line and cord Lucas had put on the rampart beside me.

I looked out to sea at the storm, now almost reaching the shore. I blew out a breath, gripped the handle of the rod, lifted it to the ten o'clock position, and waited for a break in the wind. Then with a quick movement of my arm I whipped the rod up so the line flew into the air. I held that position long enough to mouth the word *yes*, just like my dad had taught me, then shot my arm and the rod forward with all my strength.

The line flicked out exactly like it should have, but the cork hit the wall a good foot under Seneca's window. I was going to have to compensate more than I'd thought.

I set up another cast and waited for the wind to die down. It took longer this time, and the gust was the strongest so far. Every spare inch of my jacket crackled, and clumps of hair flew forward from under my hood.

No luck. I tried a third time, lifting the rod higher, and the cork hit maybe two or three inches under her window.

The wind was stronger and stronger, getting more steady now instead of gusty like before. I waited for what seemed a long time, but there wasn't a break. I glanced out to sea and saw the storm coming in. Maybe my chance for calm was over. I'd been taught how important it was for the line to flick up in the air and stay there for a beat before I sent it forward—but how could it stay up with the wind blowing it from behind?

My heart was hammering fast and my throat was dry. I was at least going to try. I got ready and, with all my strength, used the rod to toss the line into the air, but the wind was stronger than I was and the line fell maybe ten feet in front of me. I tried again. And again.

I began to panic. Had I missed my chance? If God or fate or whatever had meant for us to rescue Seneca, then it seemed like he or she or it wasn't doing a very good job of helping.

Suddenly it was calm. I breathed and lifted the rod. Then I whipped it way, way up, held it for *yes*, and threw it forward like with an overhead tennis stroke.

The line zoomed out exactly like it was supposed to. The cork shot forward, right into Seneca's window.

I imagined it landing with a soft plop in the middle of her floor.

"You rock!" Lucas said.

29
Outta There

Seneca must have seen the note on the cork, because she pulled. I pulled, too, yanking the line out from the forward end of the rod as fast as I could, keeping ahead of her. When we had enough extra yards lying around, Lucas quick cut the line with the scissors, and I knotted it to the climbing rope. Just in time, too—I'd barely finished testing the knot when Seneca pulled it out of my hands.

I kept hold, guiding the rope as Seneca pulled, slowly letting it tighten until it made a straight line from us up to the window. Meanwhile Lucas lifted up the backpack, and when we got to where it was fastened on the rope, she shifted the weight of it from her hands onto the tight line slowly enough that Seneca wouldn't let it drop on her end.

Seneca seemed to catch on, because the rope didn't sag much, even with the extra weight. The backpack went across quickly, blowing back and forth, until it got to the window slot. With all the clothes inside, it was too thick to go in the narrow opening at first, but pretty soon it seemed to get smaller—Seneca was pulling things out of it! Sweet! Finally the skinny bag disappeared into the window.

At that exact moment the storm hit us. I'd been so focused that it took me by surprise. A huge wind drove raindrops into my sore cheek so hard it was like being shot in the face with a BB gun. I screamed in pain just as Lucas yelped and grabbed my arm to keep from going over the side. Terrified we'd been heard, I looked down into the moat, but Mustache and his cell phone had disappeared.

"Are you okay?" Lucas had to shout because of the incredibly loud howling of the wind and huge crashes of the sea.

I nodded, holding my hand up to where it hurt.

We had to do a little more tying while Seneca was getting ready at her end. I did it crouched down behind the stone tooth. The rain made the rope hard to work with. I was glad for all the time I'd spent tying wet lines on boats.

When I finished, Lucas and I stayed huddled together behind the parapet. The rain was so heavy, it seemed to be seeping through our jackets and waterproof pants. It was positively pouring through the shoelace holes in my sneakers. My socks were soaked, and when I wiggled my toes, they squished around in water.

It seemed like forever, but it was probably only a couple minutes before the flickering light from Seneca's window slot was blotted out and we saw the top of her head followed by her shoulders coming sideways out of the narrow window opening.

That was my signal. The rope now led from, we hoped, something solid and unmovable in Seneca's room, across the moat to the parapet, where it hung loosely around the crenellation. I pulled it tight, knotted it securely, and threw the long, long end of it—all knotted now thanks to Lucas's work—down the outside of the wall.

Behind me, Lucas shouted, "It's a good thing she doesn't have big boobs."

I missed Seneca's chest going through, but turned in time to see her lean over, gloves on her hands, take hold of the tight rope, pull her hips and legs out of the opening, and lower them until she was hanging by her arms. Then she changed her grip and, just like she'd done on the tree branch in the cemetery, moved hand-over-hand down and across the space, holding on to the knots. Lucas's awesome idea had been that Seneca should come *across* the moat instead of down *into* it, and the idea was working perfectly! The wind was so strong it not only blew the backpack Seneca was wearing away from her body, but actually blew her whole body backward. Still, she just kept coming.

When she got close, she raised her knees and stuck out her legs to reach the rampart. We grabbed on to her and, half on her own, half thanks to us, she landed beside us. I cut the rope behind her.

It was one of the best moments of my life, having her there, the three of us hugging. I think she was crying, but it was hard to tell in the rain.

A second later she straightened. "I heard someone moving around the hall, so they might stop in to check on me," she shouted into the wind. "We'd better get out of here fast."

With Lucas in the lead, we let ourselves over the parapet to the ground and were on our way.

30

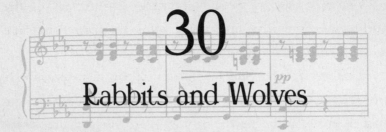

Rabbits and Wolves

We took off, leaving the way Lucas and I had come, bent over and staying closer to the shore than the path. We went as fast as we could, but between the storm hitting us head on, and our posture, and trying to run through the soaking weeds and the bushes, our progress was slow.

Too slow.

If we continued the way we were going, we would pretty soon have been so far around the side of the hill that we'd have been out of sight. But we'd gotten only about halfway to where we'd be invisible when Seneca spotted them. "They're coming!" Even though she shouted, her voice was barely loud enough to hear over the howl of the wind.

Lucas dived for cover behind the nearest bush, and I was right behind her, pulling Seneca down with me.

My heart, already pounding from the running, pumped

even faster from fear. Once on my knees, I turned to look through the bush. Green Socks and Mustache, in dark-colored rain jackets, hoods up, were on the base of the path just outside the castle, scanning the slope from side to side. Mustache raised the binoculars to his eyes.

I bit my lip and held my breath. I knew in my head he wouldn't see us. Neither he nor Green Socks had seen us earlier in the day, when the light was a lot brighter. Now the hill was blocking the daylight, it was still pouring down rain, and the clouds were as dark as ever. If our anoraks had been yellow or red, we might have been visible. But with our dark-colored jackets there was no way they could spot us from that distance, even with the binoculars.

I calmed myself down and took a deep breath. The next second, whatever safety I was feeling disappeared. Mustache yelled something at Green Socks, who began moving from one bush to another near the castle, and Mustache started up the path with his binoculars.

"He'll find us!" Even with Lucas and Seneca right beside me, I had to shout to be heard over the sound of the storm and crashing waves, the pelting rain, and the crackling and snapping of our jackets in the wind.

"No he won't!" Lucas yelled back. "We'll move around the bush as he comes up the path! Keep the bush between us and him!"

I wasn't so sure. There were three of us, and the bush wasn't that enormous. Could we lie down and be hidden in the weeds instead? But a quick glance behind me showed only a few tufts of heather sticking up in what was otherwise short grass.

My body tensed as I turned back and saw Mustache coming steadily up the path, looking with his binoculars first to one side, then to the other. It would be less than a minute, maybe not even that, before he got up even with where we were, and when he did, I was sure he'd spot an arm sticking out here or a knee there. I huddled in as tightly as I could next to Seneca and put my arm around her to get us even closer, pulling my other arm across my front, out of possible view. While I was at it, I took Seneca's hand and gripped it in mine. I was trying to stay small, hoping we could all blend into one tiny shape that might be invisible in the rain and the fading light. When she saw what I was doing, Lucas did the same thing on Seneca's other side.

Mustache, binoculars up, came closer and closer, his gaze sweeping first up the slope from the path, then downward in our direction. Then he'd stop, wipe the moisture off the lenses, take another couple steps, and do the same thing all over again. Every time the binoculars moved away from us, the three of us scooted around on our knees, clasped together in a solid pack, making sure to keep the bush between us and him. With each step, I was more and more afraid he would see us. I held my breath and squeezed Seneca's hand even harder, hoping with all my might that the raindrops streaming down the lenses of his binoculars would keep him from seeing us.

He was probably no farther away from where we were hiding than the length of the main corridor in my school when a gust of wind, as strong as any we'd felt so far, came whooshing in. Mustache was hit by both the wind and the rain. Struggling to keep his balance, he took three jerky steps backward, dropped into a crouch, pulled his hood forward with one hand, and steadied himself on the ground with the other.

When the gust let up, he got to his feet, wiped the lenses again, and took a long look around, starting on the uphill side. Then the binoculars moved down slowly, slowly in our direction.

The three of us froze. My heart was pounding, and I wanted to close my eyes, as if that would keep him from seeing us. Instead I forced myself to stare at him through the branches of the bush. Would he spot us? Were we far enough away? Were we small enough? How clear was his vision through all that water?

I held my breath as the binoculars slowly moved toward us, then at us, sure we would have to run for our lives. But his gaze went past us, and by the time the binoculars swept upward again, they were aimed a few yards beyond where we were hiding.

Mustache kept fighting his way up the hill. We watched him in silence, not moving, as he got to the top and slowly looked at every part of the slope and the curving path that we knew was in front of him. He probably spent two minutes standing there looking around before he gave up and came back down, the wind at his back pushing him into a run, the binoculars bobbing against his chest on their long strap.

At the bottom of the hill, he met up with Green Socks, who pointed at the rope dangling down the side of the battlement wall. The two guys went over to inspect it, Green Socks said something to Mustache, and the two of them walked along the wall toward the front of the castle and disappeared around the corner.

I sagged with relief, and I could feel Seneca do the same thing. Then we took off, this time straightening up and running as fast as we could around the curve and up the hill. And then, finally, we were on the path.

Relief! Not just to leave Green Socks and Mustache behind us, but to be able to trot along without tripping over the rough ground and sliding over the wet weeds and grass. Plus, by this time, it didn't seem to be blowing as hard as it had been.

But what had seemed like better weather turned out to be only a shift in the wind. The farther we got around the long curve under the big bluff, the stronger the wind got. At last the path dropped down closer to the shore, took a sharp curve to the right, and suddenly there was nothing in front of us but wind and water.

It was like having a collision with a wet mattress. The rain and the spray from the sea hit us smack in the face. Between the shrieks and bellows of the storm, and the enormous waves exploding with big booms just yards away from us, the noise was incredible.

Instead of turning back, we bent into it and struggled forward. Maybe for somebody bigger and heavier it wouldn't have been so hard, but for the three of us girls, every step was a fight against the wind. We held hands to help each other. I kept my head way down, chin on my chest. Still, the salty seawater hit me in the face and stung terribly on the thorn holes and scratches. My cheek throbbed with pain.

Moving forward was exhausting. When we came around another sharp bend, the wind caught us and blew each of us a couple of steps backward. We all sat down on our heels and huddled together for a minute to let the worst of it pass, then stood up and started again.

Step by step we pushed our way through the storm. One plod, then another, then another. Then—

"Look!" Seneca shouted. "There's a light." Sure enough, there was a fishing boat in a cove down the hill from us, shining a hugely bright spotlight up on the shore. The light moved steadily back and forth, rising higher and higher.

Suddenly Lucas yelled, "It's Green Socks and Mustache! They're after us again! Hide!" And she took off up the hill toward the nearest big bush, moving so fast that she got tangled in the first bunch of heather and almost fell. Seneca and I were right behind her.

We were almost to the bush when the light found us, making the whole hillside around us bright as day in spite of all the rain between us and the boat.

"Let's run back toward the castle," Lucas shouted. "We can find someplace to hide!"

"Look! They're coming!" Seneca's voice was full of panic.

Sure enough, two men were charging up the hill. They must have been on land before we saw the boat. It was almost dark, so we couldn't see their faces, but they were wearing dark-colored rain jackets. They were shouting something at us, but I couldn't hear it for the sound of the storm and the blood pumping in my ears.

"Run!" Lucas yelled, and we took off toward the castle.

The men were on the path now, parallel to us, sprinting with their feet on the gravel, while above them we fought through the heather and weeds with our last strength, slipping on the wet grass, the big spotlight following our every move.

Tears sprang to my eyes. It wasn't fair! We'd tried so hard! We'd gone without sleep, and been in danger, fought through a terrible storm, ended up exhausted and hungry, and I'd even kind of suffered if you counted my face. And here we were, being hunted down on a hillside in the wind and rain, like helpless little rabbits being chased by wolves. We didn't have a chance.

Sure enough, it wasn't long before the two men left the path and closed in on us, one to block our way, one below to keep us from going down or back.

The only way was up, which led to the straight, rocky wall of the bluff.

We stopped. Beaten. The guy below us, who until now had been only a shape, moved into the circle made by the always-following spotlight until we could see him clearly.

It wasn't Mustache and it wasn't Green Socks. The face under the hood of the slicker belonged to Robbie.

31
Safe and Dry

I remember the next few minutes as kind of a blur: Jamie and Robbie helping us down the steep hill into a deep, sheltered cove. The short trip in a motorized dinghy. The fishing boat, anchored in deep water where the cove widened before it met the ocean. The boat tossing up and down in the waves. The snug little cabin with its strong smell of fish. Seneca pale, teeth chattering, her whole body shaking. The twins helping her off with her coat and rain pants. Jamie pulling off our wet shoes and socks and Robbie coming behind him with dry socks he'd pulled out of a drawer under the bench seat we were sitting on. A guy about Mom's age, who seemed to own the boat, draping Seneca in blankets and telling Lucas and me to cuddle up on either side of her for warmth. Seneca, in a small voice, asking the two of us where she was, and Lucas telling her. Somebody handing me a cold, wet cloth to hold against my cheek. Jamie pumping strong tea with milk and sugar from a big thermos into tall mugs with lids. The older guy handing us sandwiches and covered mugs full of strong broth.

Being out of the rain and wind; the food; the warmth of the supercrowded cabin; the cool cloth against my throbbing, burning cheek; the older guy and the twins fussing over us while the boat pitched and bounced—it was all incredibly wonderful.

If the three men were curious about who Seneca was, what had been going on with us, or why Seneca hadn't known where she was, they didn't say so. Instead of asking us to explain anything, they seemed totally focused on feeding us and getting us warm.

It wasn't until Seneca, Lucas, and I had our tea and food and dry socks that the twins introduced the older guy as their uncle Murdo—"Call me Murdo," he said—and we introduced Seneca.

As everybody shook hands, I wondered how Murdo, who was quite amazingly short, could be the uncle of a couple of brothers who were so amazingly tall. He wore a black stocking cap and a black turtleneck under orange waterproof bibs. Every so often he looked out the windows of the cabin, and I knew he was making sure the boat wasn't drifting.

For a few seconds nobody said anything, and I figured that for sure somebody would start asking questions. I, for one, was dying to know what had happened to Seneca, but I didn't want to ask her in case she wasn't ready to talk about it.

The guys must have felt the same way about all of us, because Murdo was the only one to talk, and all he said was, "You must drink your soup. It's warrum." He had the same soft lilt his nephews had, but his voice was older and deeper.

Seneca was taking the last few drinks of broth from her covered mug, what I always think of as a grownup sippy cup. When she was done, she happened to glance in my direction. "I wanted to ask you, Kari, what happened to your face?" This what-happened-to-your-face thing was turning into a running joke.

"Um," I said, "I accidentally fell on some thistles earlier today." Before she could ask me a question about that, I said, "How did you guys find us?"

"At six o'clock, when we got off work, we went to the caff to have a bite to eat and found out you'd never been there," Robbie said. "We got worried, what with the weather blowin' in, so we went lookin' for you around the town. Along the way we met a mate of ours who said he'd seen two lassies like you turning from the lane beside the hotel onto the path to the castle."

His brother added, "We tried to get help from the police to come looking for you, but they were busy with a house fire and a car smash. So we rang Uncle Murdo, who can take his fishing boat out even in verra bad weather."

Murdo looked embarrassed. "When we saw the rain, we found a snug cove and here we are. Most times I wouldn't put in anywhere except Portree harbor in a storm like this, but we took the chance so we could look for you. It seems safe enough—we're sheltered from the worst of the storm, and so far the anchor is holding—so if we don't start to drift, we'll stay until it clears a bit."

"From here we could see you coming on the path along there," Jamie said, and pointed out the window of the cabin to a place along the shore in the distance. "We saw some wee figures all bent over, lookin' like they might need our help. We didn't know for sure it was you, because . . . because there were three of you."

As if to try to cover up the question his brother had almost asked—where did the third girl come from?—Robbie quickly said, "So Jamie and I came in the dinghy and Uncle Murdo turned the spotlight on the shore. Then you thought we were up to no good, and you ran away from us."

Lucas had heard the question that hadn't been asked. She's not always as sensitive about other people's feelings as I am, or as the twins and their uncle seemed to be, so she launched right in, saying, "I think it's probably time for us to tell our story—or stories, since we have one and Seneca has her own. If you're wondering how we managed to go out to the castle with two girls and come back with a third one . . . well, the reason is that Seneca was kidnapped after playing a concert at the Edinburgh Festival on Friday night. The kidnappers hid her at the castle. When you saw us on the path, we were coming back after rescuing her."

The three guys just stared at us for a minute, but Seneca didn't seem to realize how weird all this had sounded, because she just nodded and said, "I can't believe you guys found me. How did you do it?"

She wasn't shivering anymore, and Lucas and I weren't sitting quite as close to her as we had been, but I noticed that she kept the blankets around her.

"It's kind of complicated," Lucas said. "Maybe you'd better begin with the part where you were kidnapped and we'll get to the rescue after that."

As badly as I wanted to hear Seneca tell her story, I said, "Don't feel like you have to say anything if you don't want to."

"No, that's okay. I can talk about it."

The twins were sitting on the bench across from us by this time, their uncle standing beside them where he could keep glancing out the window. All three of them looked surprised and almost confused.

Seneca said, "I'm a pianist, and I was playing a concert with Orchestra Pacifica on Friday night at the Usher Hall in Edinburgh. When I went back to my dressing room after my performance, two guys jumped at me and grabbed me. One of them held me while the other one put my hoodie on me like you'd put a jacket on a little kid. At first I tried to fight them. I'm pretty strong for a girl my age, but I wasn't as strong as they were. Finally I just quit fighting. Later, I learned their names were Ross and Donny."

"We've been calling them Green Socks and Mustache," I said.

"I heard you use those names back on the path, when we thought they were chasing us. Green Socks would be Donny. He always wears green. Ross has a big mustache."

Lucas said, "I just thought of something. Shouldn't we call the police and get them looking for those guys?"

"They've been askin' those of us out in our boats not to use our ship-to-shore radio in this storm unless we're calling for a rescue," Uncle Murdo said. He pulled a cell phone out of his pocket and flipped it open. "No mobile reception here, but we can call as soon as we're nearing Portree. I think this storm will be over soon, and we can go back to the harbor. Are you certain the two men know you're gone?"

Seneca was taking a sip of tea, so Lucas answered. "Yes, they chased us, but we hid behind one of those evergreen bushes that grow around here, whatever they are."

"Gorse," Murdo said. "Well, don't you be worryin'. The only way off the island in an automobile is over the bridge, and it will take them a good hour to get there— probably more, in this weather. And aside from that, they'll have to pack up their things, in order not to leave evidence for the police. We'll be able to call in plenty of time for the island constabulary to catch them. Seneca, let's hear the rest of your story."

Seneca started talking again, her voice sounding automatic, like what she was telling us was a dream she'd had instead of something she'd actually been through.

Ross and Donny had dumped her into the violin crate and hauled her out to the van. She spent the night on the crate's foam liner with a packing quilt to cover her up. It was cold, the ride was rough, and she was terrified, so she hardly slept at all.

By the time they got to the castle, it was morning. They marched her inside, through the part of the building that was being worked on, which had canvases hanging over most of the walls and a lot of tools sitting around, then through a part of the castle that was nothing but stone—walls, floors, ceilings, pillars—and stone arches or heavy wooden doors leading into bare rooms.

A lot of the doors were rotting, but the door to her room was solid. There was no furniture inside it. Her bed was the piece of foam from the bottom of the crate, plus the packing quilt and one smelly blanket. They gave her a pair of men's wool socks. Otherwise her only clothes were her concert gown and hoodie—not even a pair of pajamas. It was all so uncomfortable she hardly slept again the second night. She had a space heater with an extension cord that ran under her door. The light in her room was from a lantern. Three times a day they brought her bread, cheese, and water. To keep from getting bored, she practiced piano in her head.

After she had told us all of this, she said, "The one

good thing that happened after we got to the castle was that Donny and Ross told me over and over again that they weren't going to hurt me. And they weren't really being mean to me, so I wasn't as terrified as I'd been on the ride up.

"Anyway, I thought it was probably about time for them to bring my evening bread and cheese when I heard a noise that turned out to be pebbles hitting the glass. I opened my window, and suddenly this plastic thread thing came flying into my room with a little cork and a note on it that said, *Pull*."

Everybody turned to look at Lucas and me, and Lucas said, "It was fishing line. Kari cast it across with a fishing pole—"

"Fly rod," I corrected.

"With a fly rod," Lucas said. "It was seriously cool the way she did it."

Murdo had been looking more and more astonished. "Where were you two lasses when this happened?"

"You know that wall that surrounds the moat?" Lucas asked. "With the battlements?"

The three guys all nodded in silence.

"Well, we were on the rampart."

"In this storm?" Murdo pronounced it *storrum*.

"Well actually, when I was casting, it was only windy," I said. "It didn't really start storming until right before Seneca came across on the rope. We'd tied the fishing line to some climbing rope, so the rope went over when Seneca pulled."

"I can't believe you guys did all of this to help me," Seneca said. "You were so brave! And it was so dangerous. I don't even know how to say thank you."

"You don't need to say thank you," I said. "You're our friend. Of course we had to help you."

"And you were just as brave as we were!" Lucas said. She turned to the guys. "Seneca came across hand over hand. We saw her do it in Edinburgh on a tree in a grave-yard, so we knew she could."

"In a graveyard?" Robbie said, not so much as a ques-tion, but more like it sounded absolutely incredible to him.

"You should have seen her coming across that moat!" Lucas continued. "The wind was so bad by then that it was even blowing in the moat, so her body was swaying, and the rain was pelting down, and she just came over, like it was easy. It was awesome! She was superbrave!"

"I was brave, wasn't I?" Seneca said, and gave the tini-est of smiles. She turned back to the men, with the first sparkle I'd seen in her eyes that night. "You know, I'm actually part Scottish."

If anything, the guys looked even more surprised than they'd been before.

"Seriously. Even if I don't look like a Scot. My mother is half Scottish. Scottish people are supposed to have a lot of courage. When I was coming across the moat, I was singing "Scotland the Brave" to myself, and keeping time with my grips on the rope." She started humming that tune she loved so much, marking the rhythm as she gestured the hand-over-hand movement we'd seen her use less than an hour before.

Maybe it was just because I was totally exhausted, or maybe it was because we'd been through so much that day, or maybe it was something else, but I got tears in my eyes listening to the tune and watching her.

"You are a credit to all the Scots," Murdo said, and I thought I saw his eyes filling up a little bit, too.

The twins just sat there, *their* eyes wide and their mouths open, as if they were so surprised at the story they'd heard that they were speechless. Murdo shook his head, probably in disbelief, turned to us, and said, "Now let's hear about you two lassies! It sounds as if you have an extraordinary tale to tell as well."

The storm seemed to be clearing a little, and it wouldn't be long until we could go. So Lucas and I told our story in a hurry, one talking for a while, then the other. As it happened, I was the one who ended up telling about finding Seneca gone at intermission, and Parker and the "dollhouse castle in the sky." I wasn't sure, after all she'd been through, that Seneca was ready to talk about her tutor arranging for her kidnapping, so I on purpose didn't say anything about the tarot card.

When I got to the part about trying to contact Mom, I said, "And for some reason we haven't been able to reach my mother on her cell phone." Which wasn't exactly a lie.

"Spotty mobile reception in some parts of the Highlands," Robbie muttered.

"Ah," I said, and nodded. Again, it wasn't exactly a lie.

Lucas must have gotten my hint from all of this, because when it was her turn to talk again, she shot me a Look, then explained how we learned about Old Dalhousie Castle at the tourist office, and the trip to Portree, all without mentioning anything about Paul and Edie.

Then it was my turn to talk again. I told about being at the castle that morning—I made sure to mention that we'd seen a white van outside the castle, so Uncle Murdo could tell the police—and ended up with my dive into the thistles.

"Dreadful thing, the Scottish thistle," Murdo said.

"You can say that again," I muttered.

Lucas said, "After that we came back into town and figured out our plan for casting the line into Seneca's room, and bought all the stuff we needed, including the fly line and fly rod." I was glad she didn't call it a fishing pole. "And that's about the time you saw us," she finished, looking at the twins. "Thank you, guys, by the way. I don't know what we would have done if you hadn't been there."

"Yeah, thank you *so much*!" I said.

"That's quite the story," Murdo said, ignoring our thanks. I think he was a little embarrassed.

"I still can't believe all you have done for me," Seneca

said, and now she was the one getting tears in her eyes.

Murdo looked at her and said in a gentle voice, "Well, you must all be verra exhausted."

Having him say this made me realize just how tired I was. With all my might I wanted to take a nice hot shower and snuggle into bed. And suddenly it struck me that I was feeling like a little kid: I wanted my mom.

Murdo opened the cabin door, stuck his head out into what was now darkness, and said, "I think we can start back noo."

All three guys put on their rain jackets and went outside.

As for my feelings about Robbie—well, somehow, knowing how ugly I was with my cheek red and swollen and my hair soaked, and thinking about the beautiful Polish girl who was his age, it was like a switch had been turned off and I didn't feel self-conscious or fluttery or anything. He was still a cute guy, and yeah, if I'd been a little older I might still have had a thing for him. But as it was, he and Jamie had been acting like we were their little sisters, and I was just fine with that.

Seneca got out of her seat for the first time and watched vaguely out the window as the twins brought the anchor up and the boat, now with its motor on, turned toward the open water.

She was totally silent until we were safely in the water *put-putting* our way toward Portree. Then she turned to us and said, "Did you figure out the clue I managed to smuggle out of the dressing room?"

"The tarot card?" Lucas asked.

She nodded.

"We, um . . ." I didn't know quite what to say about this. "We figured you might mean that Edie was in on it in some way."

"That's exactly what I meant," Seneca said. "But it wasn't just Edie. Paul was in on it, too."

32

What Seneca Saw, and the Surprise in the Hotel Room

Lucas and I glanced at each other, but Seneca's eyes were blazing with anger, and we didn't interrupt.

"I knew she had arranged to have me kidnapped the minute I went backstage at intermission and saw the two guys waiting for me. Remember before the concert, when I was using your opera glasses?"

We nodded, and she told us about seeing Edie talking to the guy she thought was a taxi driver, but who turned out to be Donny.

"We figured out the same thing," I said.

"How?" Seneca asked.

"Um, it had to do with guys wearing green—"

Lucas interrupted. "It's a long story. But tell us what made you think Paul was in on it."

"It was when I was in my dressing room at the Usher Hall. The concert was about to begin. Mom and Paul and Edie were leaving my room to take their seats. Mom hugged me—she always hugs me for luck before a concert—and while she had her arms around me, I randomly looked toward one of the pictures on the wall and saw Paul and Edie reflected in the glass.

"The reflection was perfect. Edie kissed her hand and touched it to his cheek. Then they bumped fists. The whole thing took only a few seconds. When Mom and I turned back to them, they had their old expressions, as if nothing had happened.

"It didn't make any sense to me at the time, but when I thought about it later and remembered that guy who looked like a taxi driver . . ." She trailed off and shrugged.

"You knew they were in it together," I said.

Now that the boat wasn't protected by the shores of the cove, it was heaving up and down in the water, the wind blowing the waves right at us. But we were finally getting close to Portree harbor. Seneca, her face still set with anger, raised her head and looked through the rain at the lighted buildings along the pier and on the hills of the town.

Then she turned back to us. "I figured it all out lying in the crate in the van that night. Paul and Edie were having an affair, and they wanted to take all the money they could from Mom and me. In a way, that's why Donny and Ross didn't hurt me. Paul and Edie needed me to come back safe. They'd end up with the money from my kidnapping, and when the story got out about what happened to me, I'd suddenly become really famous, and the amount they could charge for me to play concerts would go up, so they could make more money that way, too."

I looked at Lucas. "So *that's* why they wanted Mom to be there right after the kidnapping—so she could write a big feature story about it!"

Lucas nodded. "Makes sense," she said, and explained to Seneca about the scene in the dressing room reminding me of that Agatha Christie play, and how mad Paul and Edie had been when my mom wasn't there to see what happened that night.

"Anyway," Seneca continued, "after they'd been hauling in the big concert fees for a few months or maybe a year and that kidnapping thing wasn't news anymore, Paul would leave my mom for Edie, and the two of them could live it up on our money for the rest of their lives."

"Paul is such a total bag of pus, I'll bet he even negotiated a contract so he'd be able to keep getting part of your concert fees no matter what."

Seneca sighed. "I wouldn't be surprised. Mom is so crazy about him that she'd sign anything he told her to. This is going to be terrible for her." She looked down, and for the second time that night I saw tears in her eyes.

A minute later she took a big breath and said, "Anyway, you probably noticed that I didn't ask Jamie or Robbie or their uncle to use their cell phone to call my mom to tell her I was okay."

I hadn't thought about it, but now that she mentioned it, I suppose that was kind of weird.

"That's because I didn't want Mom to tell Paul and Edie that I'd been found before I have a chance to talk to the police and tell them what's *really* going on."

"We'll have to go to the police station tonight when we get back to shore," Lucas said.

I felt like groaning. I thought of all we'd been through that day. The path to the castle was two and a half miles one way, so Lucas and I had walked probably nine miles total, the last mile and a half or so through a terrible storm. We'd fought the wind up on the rampart. We'd been out in the cold all day, lying around on the ground, and I'd been terrified half the time, which made the experience even worse. Plus I had the pain from the thistles. I was so exhausted that just the thought of dragging myself up the steep hill from the harbor to the hotel seemed like it would kill me, but at least I'd be heading for a shower, dry pajamas, and a warm bed. Now it looked like we were going to have to haul ourselves up the hill just to spend an hour or two or even more at the Portree police station.

"Then we can tell them why Kari and I knew Paul was in on it," Lucas said.

"So you knew he was guilty before I even told you?"

Lucas and I nodded.

"How did you know?"

"We just saw and heard some things," Lucas said.

"Do you have proof?" she asked, looking from one of us to the other.

"Maybe," I said. "I mean, we don't exactly have the proof ourselves, but I think the police may be able to prove it. Paul made a phone call to Portree on his cell phone. That might be the best evidence. If the police can prove that he called somebody who might be connected with the crime, maybe someone who had something to do with the work they're doing on the castle, then I think they'll have the evidence they need. Besides, Green Socks and Mustache would probably testify against Paul and Edie."

Just then Robbie opened the door of the cabin and stuck his head in. "Mrs. MacLeod just called my mobile. Kari's mum is at the hotel."

I was so exhausted that it took me a second to even understand what Robbie had just said. When I did, I smiled a big smile, and it was all I could do not to give out a hoot. Mom had come, and she was waiting for us! I could hardly believe it.

Robbie continued, "And Uncle Murdo reached the police, and they're looking for the two criminals in their van. But they need to have you come to the station to make statements when you've changed into dry clothes. We'll go down and speak with the constable on duty as soon as we get the boat tied down, and you and your mum can join us there later."

We were close to the shore by that time, but I was so anxious to see Mom that the last *put-put-putting* to get to the dock seemed to take forever.

We went up on deck, waited until the boat was tied down, then took off for the hotel.

It was dark and, although the wind wasn't as strong as it had been, the rain was still pouring down. But I didn't care about the dark, didn't care about the weather, didn't care about how much my legs ached or notice how exhausted I was as I climbed the steep hill. Mom was there, and that was all that mattered.

When we walked through the door into the hotel, Mrs. MacLeod said in a sour voice, "I suppose the twins told you your mum has arrived. And not before time. She's in your room."

It didn't matter to me whether or not Mrs. MacLeod approved of us. I ran up the stairs, Seneca and Lucas behind me, raced down the hall, and flung the door open.

Edie was sitting on the bed. She dropped the magazine she was reading and scrambled to her feet without bothering to slip back into her stilettos. Her too-loud voice said, "Thank God you're safe!"

33

Seneca Has Enough

I stood there stunned, my hand on the door handle. Edie brushed past me, threw her arms around Seneca, and pulled her into the room.

The door to the bathroom was open. I walked over and glanced inside for Mom, but the bathroom was empty.

"Where's Gillian?" Lucas asked, as Seneca squirmed out of Edie's hug.

"Gillian?" Edie asked. She stepped behind Lucas and closed the door. "Gillian's not here. I said I was Kari's mother so they'd let me in the room."

The disappointment hit me like a punch to the stomach.

"Did you call her and say you'd found out where we were?" Lucas asked.

"Not yet." She sent a look toward Seneca, who was calmly looking back at her. "I, um, wanted to be able to tell her I'd found you safe. Are you okay, Seneca? Who kidnapped you? And where did they take you? How did you escape? I want to be able to tell Paul and your mother all about what happened."

Seneca stayed silent. Lucas stepped forward as if ready to take charge, but Seneca raised a hand as if to say that *she* was going to be the boss here, and she had it all under control.

Without taking her eyes off Edie's face, she said, "I think it's more important that we catch the guys who kidnapped me. Let's call the police now so I can give them a description and they can get a search started."

Too tired to think straight, I actually opened my mouth to say something about the police already looking for the kidnappers. Lucas poked me with her elbow, and I closed my mouth, wondering what Seneca was up to.

Edie pulled her cell phone out of the pocket of her black pantsuit. "First I'm going to call Paul and Teresa. They've been frantic."

"I'm asking you to call the police," Seneca said. Her eyes were narrowed, and to me she looked dangerous, but her voice sounded totally calm. "In case you've forgotten, *I'm* the one who was kidnapped, not you, not my mother, not Paul. I'm telling you, I know who the kidnappers are and I don't want them to get away."

Edie was punching numbers into the cell phone. "Your mother is in a panic, Seneca. I need to call her first. And we want Kari's mother to start the journey here. Let me just take care of this." She lifted the phone to her ear.

Seneca was smaller and at least four inches shorter than Edie, but she reached out, pulled at Edie's hand, and the phone fell to the floor. Then she moved in close to her.

"You don't *want* Donny and Ross to get caught, do you?" Her teeth were clenched now, and she spoke directly into Edie's face.

Edie moved her head back a little to get space between her and Seneca. "Why would you say a thing like that?" she said, trying to make her expression look pleasant and puzzled.

"Because if they're caught, they'll tell the police that you and Paul hired them!" Seneca said. This time her face was stuck in so close that Edie took a step backward.

Seneca moved in on Edie, who backed away again. "You had me kidnapped so that you and Paul could take the money that belongs to Mom and me and go away together! Do you know what this is going to do to my mother?" Seneca continued, and took another step. "You're evil, that's what you are. Both you and Paul are *evil*!"

"Why are you making these crazy accusations?" Edie's too-loud laugh sounded definitely nervous.

"Don't try to act innocent! We know all about it!" Seneca took one last step forward, forcing Edie up against the wall. "And what *you* don't know is that the police are *already* looking for Donny and Ross!"

Edie looked from Lucas to me with panic in her eyes,

as if to see whether what Seneca had just said was true. Then, with a movement as quick as a striking snake, she spun Seneca around and pulled her close, arm around her waist. With her other hand she grabbed Seneca's wrist and twisted. Seneca grimaced and yelled in pain.

"You two so much as move a muscle, and I'll twist Seneca's arm until something snaps or breaks. Do you understand that?" Edie's mouth was pulled back in a snarl.

Lucas and I nodded slowly and stood where we were, frozen in place. A broken arm or a snapped tendon would be painful for anybody, but for Seneca it could be terrible for her career.

Edie's eyes darted from Lucas to me, then back to Lucas. "So, you have it all figured out," she said through clenched teeth, and edged away from the wall. "I figured you knew more than was good for you when I saw you getting on that train at Waverley Station. I guess I underestimated just how *much* you knew."

She hesitated a second and took a breath, as if making a quick decision. "Okay, you're just going to have to undo the damage you've already done. One of you is going to go to that telephone over there, call the hotel operator, and ask for the police station. When they connect you, you're going to tell the police that you talked to Kari's mother when you got back to the room, and you confessed to her that whatever you said that got them searching for the kidnappers was a pack of lies.

"You're going to say that the three of you girls arranged for Seneca to leave Edinburgh and pretend it was a kidnapping—"

She never had a chance to finish. Seneca, bottom lip shoved up in a fierce expression, raised her foot and brought her boot heel down as hard as she could on Edie's bare instep. Edie let out a scream, and Seneca, wrist now free, rammed her elbow into Edie's side with all the strength of her arms and shoulders.

Quick-thinking Lucas landed Edie a karate kick to her hip as she fell. Once she hit the floor, I jumped on top of her, knees in her stomach. Edie, obviously crazy with anger, reached up, put her hands around my throat, and started to squeeze.

"Take your hands off my daughter!"

I raised my eyes to where the voice had come from. Mom was standing in the doorway, her friend Celia and Mrs. MacLeod right behind her.

34
Lucas and Jamie and Josh

It was almost midnight. Edie was in jail. Green Socks and Mustache had been caught as they crossed the bridge. Seneca and Lucas and I, plus Celia and Mom, had spent hours telling our stories to Constable Bennie, the police constable on duty. I'd also brought along my list of clues and deductions, which the constable seemed to think was pretty good. And yes, the twins and Uncle Murdo had told their stories, too, but theirs were shorter than ours, so it hadn't taken as long.

Constable Bennie wouldn't tell us anything about when the cops were going to arrest Paul, but we figured it must be going to happen that night, because they told Seneca she'd be able to talk to her mother in the morning. Also in the morning, the three of us girls would travel with Celia, Mom, and the constable to Edinburgh, where we'd have to spend a whole bunch more hours telling our stories to a whole bunch more policemen. I figured that by the time it was over, telling our stories was going to get seriously old.

But first the cops were going to let us get some sleep. We were in the room with Mom, and Seneca and Celia were next door with, of all things, a social worker who'd been assigned to take care of Seneca. Our lights were still on—Mom was taking her shower—but Lucas, lying next to me, looked like she might fall asleep any minute. Before she did, there was a question I had to have answered.

"Lucas, about Robbie and Jamie."

"What about them?"

"How did you end up feeling about Jamie?"

Lucas sat up, turned, and plumped her pillow, then lay down again, looking at me. "I guess . . . if I were older, I'd still like him. But I'm not older, so I . . . I kind of gave up."

"I know what you mean. That sounds like the same way I ended up feeling about Robbie."

We were quiet again. This time it was Lucas who talked. "But Jamie made me feel . . . different."

"Different how?"

"Different about Josh," she said at last. She rolled from her side onto her back and stared up at the ceiling. "I haven't told you, but in all the time we've been here, I haven't gotten one single solitary e-mail from him."

"I wondered about that. I thought you'd probably have told me if you did."

"Remember that bus ride in the rain when we were on our way to Portree?"

I nodded.

"Well, the whole time, I was making excuses for him. Reasons he might not write. Like he had a cold or whatever."

I nodded.

"But then I met Jamie, and he was so cute and talked so nice and everything, but he also *was* nice. And he's kind of serious and smart, but brave, too. And I thought, if *he'd* liked me for a while, maybe he would have kept *on* liking me. And he would have sent me an e-mail. . . ."

She turned to look at me, as if she wondered if I understood what she was saying. She wasn't really making sense, but I thought I knew what she meant—that she wanted a better kind of guy and somebody who liked her back—and I nodded.

"I . . ." She closed her eyes. "I don't think Josh likes me anymore."

I wanted to say, *No meep, Sherlock.* But I managed to keep my mouth shut.

"And I'm upset about that, but meeting Jamie helped me be *less* upset. Because Jamie's more the kind of boyfriend I'd like to have. I don't think I'd even *want* Josh to be my boyfriend anymore, even if he wanted to be. Which he wouldn't."

This was absolutely huge. I wanted to shout *Hooray* and get up and do a little dance in the middle of the hotel room. I wondered if I should hug her, but I was saved from having to decide because Mom came out of the bathroom.

35

Getting Hardly Mentioned in the Paper, and Mom, *My* Mom, Quotes Garth Brooks

"Oh, and here's where they mention you," Mom said, shaking out the *Scotsman* newspaper she was reading. "At the very end of the article. 'Two minors assisted with the rescue and with the capture of one of the suspects.'"

Seconds passed. "That's *it*?" Lucas asked. "That's all the credit they gave us?"

Mom nodded, laid down the newspaper, pushed her glasses up to the top of her head, and reached for another piece of toast.

I felt practically insulted. "*Assisted* with the rescue. *Assisted* with the capture of Edie. *Assisted*? *We* did it! All of it, except for Seneca's part. The police didn't have one single thing to do with it!"

"Bummer," Mom said, and spread her toast with marmalade. "I have to hand it to you, what you two did was absolutely extraordinary."

She stopped spreading and raised her knife in the air. "Incredibly dangerous, mind you, but utterly extraordinary." She put her knife down and took a bite of her toast. Practically from the minute she'd found me sitting on top of Edie and Edie trying to choke me, she'd been going on and on and on about how dangerous the things we'd done had been, and all the terrible things that could have happened to us. But I have to admit, to be fair to her, that she gave us credit for figuring out what to do and how to do it, and for all our courage and hard work.

We'd driven into Edinburgh the day before. Now it was Tuesday morning, and we were back where it had all started—for me, at least—sitting at the sidewalk café outside our Edinburgh hotel, the exact same place where we'd first met Parker. Inside was the coffee shop where I'd seen Paul slam his cell phone on the table. I couldn't believe all that had happened only a week before.

"Maybe they don't give names of minors for the same reason they only said Paul and Edie and Donny and Ross had been charged in the crime, but not what each one of them had actually done," Mom said. "Libel laws."

"What's libel?" I asked, and picked up my hot chocolate.

"It means writing something that's not true that makes somebody look bad. Scottish law is different from English law, but at least in England, once a person is charged with a crime, the media have to be very careful what they say about them, because anything they say might ruin the reputation of the defendant if that defendant ends up being found not guilty."

"There's no way *these* defendants will be found not guilty!" Lucas said, and brushed away a bug that had landed on her arm. "Look at all the evidence the cops have against them! Seneca's going to testify against Donny and Ross, and Donny and Ross are going to testify against Paul and Edie, right?"

Mom nodded and poured herself another cup of coffee. "That's what I understand."

"And then they have Paul's cell phone with the call to that construction guy they talked about in the article, the one who let them use the room in the castle and who was a friend of Ross and Donny," I said.

"And they have all those messages Edie sent to Celia's phone, pretending they were from you," Mom said, sounding guilty and glum.

I put my empty cup down on the table. "Don't blame yourself, Mom. It wasn't your fault!"

She'd really felt bad about staying out of touch for so long when we needed her help so badly. She hadn't known we were in trouble until Sunday evening when she was waiting for Celia to get ready to go out to dinner and randomly decided to open her computer and check her e-mail. (By the way, she told us that the password on her e-mail account was *Guido*, the name of our cat. I never would've thought of trying *Guido*.)

It turned out to be just like I'd suspected. Edie had been the one who took the phone Mom had left for *us*, and had used it to send texts to Celia's number with messages supposedly from me and exactly like something I'd write. One said, "gr8 time. s having fun with l and me. sidewalk shows 2day. ruok? miss u. luv." Another said, "u r at loch ness? hcit? having fun. art museum 2day. hi 2 c. luv."

The idea of Edie looking back through my old messages so she could copy them really creeped me out. It was like finding out somebody had been rooting through my underwear drawer. And poor Celia—who, by the way, had left for London very early in the morning so she could prepare for the client meeting, which had been rescheduled for the next day—was going to have to buy a new phone because the police were keeping hers as evidence.

"Anyway, back to the point," Mom said. "I'm guessing the libel laws are the reason your names aren't in the paper."

"Stinks," Lucas said. "Still, I'm not sure we want to go through the whole famous-for-our-part-of-it thing again. We had enough of that after Amsterdam."

"Come to think of it, you're right," I said.

"But what about the story I'm going to write about Seneca and the kidnapping? You don't want to be in it? Have the world know how smart and brave you were?"

Lucas and I looked at each other and shook our heads. "I don't want to be interviewed by the newspapers and TV people again," I said. "All our friends made such a big deal about it after the Lucretia thing. The second time, it would be embarrassing."

"Yeah, people would make fun of us. Keep us out of it."

"Might be better that way, actually. It was bad enough having the world know that I let you get into trouble over *The Third Lucretia*. If they learn that you traveled all the way from Edinburgh to Skye and rescued Seneca from a castle without me even knowing about it, the child protection people would probably come and take you away."

Because of the way magazines work, it would be a couple of months before Mom's story was published. That gave Teresa more time to recover. She was taking it hard. She'd already been through a whole lot—not just the kidnapping of her daughter, but finding out that the man she was nuts about had been responsible for it. Plus that he'd had a girlfriend. And Teresa still had a lot of tough stuff to get through. The news of the kidnapping was sure to come out in America—maybe it already had, although it hadn't been in the *Herald Tribune* yet. We'd checked. Mom said she'd do a Google news search later that day.

As you can imagine, what with the fact that she hadn't had a chance to practice for days, plus everything that was going on with her mother, Seneca wasn't going to be playing any more concerts at the festival. After all the time we'd spent talking to the police over the past two days, the cops seemed to think they had all the information they needed for the time being, so they said it would be okay for Seneca and her mom to fly back to their home in New

York today. The two of them were upstairs packing.

It would have been okay if they had come to breakfast with us, but it was kind of nice to be sitting at the outdoor table alone with Lucas and Mom. It felt so kind of *regular* after all the surreal things we'd been through ever since Friday night.

We had an hour and a half to kill before Teresa and Seneca would be all packed and ready to leave, so we walked up the Royal Mile and saw a bunch of Festival sidewalk performances.

It was a beautiful day—the first totally sunny day we'd had since before leaving for Skye. The best act we saw was a blond guy in dreadlocks playing this, like, seven-foot-long hugely bass-note instrument Mom said was a didgeridoo, which is an Australian instrument. The sound was weird, but he was really good and got a lot of tips.

After that we went to Princes Street Gardens, which runs right through the middle of the city. We found a bench where we could hear the bagpiper playing on the corner and just sat listening, feeling the sunshine and looking at the flowers and the incredible view of Edinburgh rising on the hill in front of us, with Edinburgh Castle at the top.

We'd been there for a while without talking when Mom said, "Lucas, over the past two days I haven't heard you mention anything about Josh Daniels. Something up with that?"

Lucas leaned forward with her hands propped at the edge of the bench, looked down, and swung her feet back and forth.

Finally she took a big breath and said, "Yeah. It's over. I thought he had a thing for me, but I guess he really didn't."

"Does that hurt?"

Lucas nodded. "Yeah, it does. But I decided I want somebody better. And somebody who likes me more than Josh ever did."

"That's good, Lucas. You need somebody truly special, because you're pretty much in a class by yourself. I'm not sure Josh was that person."

"I wish I'd never liked him."

"There's a line from a song you might want to think about. The singer's girlfriend has said good-bye, and the line goes, 'I could have missed the pain, but I'd of had to miss the dance.' That's a good way to think about these things, even when they hurt."

"Who sang it?" Lucas asked.

I expected Mom to say somebody like Frank Sinatra or Marvin Gaye, but instead she said, "Garth Brooks."

If I hadn't been sitting between Mom and Lucas, I think I would have fallen sideways. On a good day, my mother, the original classical, jazz, and R & B fan might admit there was something *called* country music. The idea that she not only knew who Garth Brooks was but also knew the lyrics to one of his songs totally blew me away.

If Lucas was surprised, she didn't show it. She just kept leaning on her hands, swinging her feet.

"I get that, kind of," she said. "But it wasn't much of a dance, when you come right down to it. Every time I think about it, I feel stupid."

"When it comes to romance, we all end up feeling stupid once in a while. Like the song says, it's part of the dance, part of the texture of life."

I was afraid for a minute that what with all this Part of the Dance and Texture of Life business, Mom would say next that Lucas was a Woman with a Past, and if that happened, I'd have to go over to the bushes and throw up.

Lucas saved me by saying, "I don't know why I got so, you know, totally obsessed about him."

"It's a chemical phenomenon, Lucas. That obsession is not just *like* a drug, it actually *is* a drug. Drugs, actually. We call our feeling infatuation, but there are real scientific names for the stuff in our brain that makes us feel that way. Dopamine and norepinephrine. They take over for a while. In all of us sometimes. I've been through it. Kari will go through it." Mom looked at me, smiled, and raised her eyebrows. "If she's lucky."

Lucas turned to me. "When you go through it, I hope you don't end up feeling as stupid as I do."

"When I go through it, I hope I don't either," I said. But I wondered about that look of Mom's, and I remembered the way I had felt about Robbie. Maybe there was something to this dance business after all.

36
Finale

Saying good-bye to Seneca and Teresa started out being hard. I was feeling really sad about having Seneca leave— we'd gotten to be really close friends in a supershort time because of all the things we'd been through together.

Teresa looked like she'd been crying all morning, and there were such big circles under her eyes that I wondered if she'd slept at all. Seneca was being really nice to her. Somehow it seemed like the relationship between them had changed. Seneca seemed like she'd gotten a lot older over the past couple of days, and now she was taking care of her mother instead of the other way around.

We hadn't been talking long before Seneca looked at Lucas and me and said, "Mom and I have made a decision. We want the two of you to join Gillian when she comes to New York City to hear me play Carnegie Hall. You'll be our guests for the trip. It will be our way of saying thank you for everything you did to rescue me. Please say you will! It will mean so much to me—well, to both of us."

So on Saturday, Lucas, Mom, and I flew home from Edinburgh, and exactly two weeks later we caught another plane and flew from the Minneapolis–Saint Paul airport to New York City. We were barely on the plane, Lucas and I still busy settling in with our iPods, when Mom turned a page in the *New York Times* she had been reading and said, "Hey, you guys, look at this!"

There was a photo of Seneca beside a story with the headline RECENTLY KIDNAPPED PIANIST ANNOUNCES CAREER HIATUS. The story began:

> Celebrated piano prodigy Seneca Crane, 15, today announced a three-year suspension of her concert career. Ms. Crane was abducted last month from her dressing room at Edinburgh's famed Usher Hall immediately following her critically acclaimed performance with Orchestra Pacifica at the prestigious Edinburgh International Festival. She was held for two days in a medieval castle in a remote section of Scotland before escaping.
>
> Paul R. Didier, Ms. Crane's stepfather and manager, and her tutor, Edith A. Francis, have been arrested and charged with masterminding the abduction. Two Scottish men are also being held in connection with the case.
>
> Ms. Crane's temporary retirement will be ef-

fective following a series of appearances for which she had been previously contracted, concluding in February with a final concert with the Atlanta Symphony Orchestra. Her statement was released to the press in conjunction with her appearance tonight at Carnegie Hall as guest soloist with Orchestra Pacifica. The performance caps the ensemble's three-week European tour.

Lucas and I looked at each other. "So she did it!" Lucas said.

"Good for her!" I said.

Seneca and her mom were waiting for us when we got to the hotel, and as soon as we had taken our suitcases up to our room and unpacked the clothes we were going to wear to the concert that night, we all went to lunch together.

Sitting at the table with Seneca and her mom, I couldn't help thinking about the meals we'd had with them when Paul and Edie had been around. I wondered if Teresa and Seneca were thinking the same thing.

Teresa still seemed shaky, but she was a ton better than she'd been when we said good-bye to her in Edinburgh. Seneca was wired thinking about the concert that night, but I could tell there had been changes in her. It's hard to describe. There was something kind of *solid* about her now that hadn't been there before.

I noticed that neither one of them said anything about the announcement we'd seen in the paper. But when Lucas, Seneca, and I went off to the bathroom together, Seneca said, "Did you see the article in the *New York Times* today?"

We nodded. "That is so cool!" I said.

"Congratulations!" Lucas added.

Seneca smiled, showing her dimples. "I'm so excited! And it was easier than I expected. Mom wasn't as upset as I thought she was going to be. She was *really* not looking forward to meeting up with all her old friends in the music business and having them know that she had fallen in love with and *married* the guy who ended up having her daughter kidnapped.

"Next week we're moving to Atlanta. She's really close to my aunt who lives there, even though Auntie Zee was my father's sister. Mom's already calling around to see if she can get a job teaching piano at one of the colleges there. I hope she can settle in and have a nice, normal life for a change.

"And of course, I'll be able to hang out with LaToya. I'm going to go to her high school and everything. I can't wait!"

The concert was, like they say, a huge sensation. The story about the kidnapping had been on cable TV and in all the papers for about a week, with reporters digging up everything they could about everybody involved, especially Paul and Edie.

So what with that and the announcement that this was the last concert Seneca was going to play in New York for at least three years, it was no big surprise that the crowd was enormous. Carnegie Hall has a lot of seats and a bunch of balconies, just like the Usher Hall. There were people standing all over the back, and every single balcony was full. It wasn't hard to see that Paul had been right when he thought that being kidnapped would help Seneca attract bigger audiences.

We sat in a box seat in the First Tier, right above the stage on what Mom calls the "piano side," which is the side where you can see the pianist's fingers on the keyboard. I'd never sat in a box before. This one had eight chairs, and there was a low wall separating us from the next box over. It was the fanciest place I've ever sat at a concert in my whole life.

Teresa was with us, and guess who else was there: Parker! He was cuter than ever, dressed in nice slacks, a white shirt, and a bow tie. He'd been excited to find out we were coming to the concert, and his parents said that when they'd told him he could sit with us, he'd clapped his hands and laughed. Which made me want to clap *my* hands and laugh.

Before the concert, Lucas and I got down on the floor with him and played trucks. He'd moved on from *vroom*

vroom and now rolled his trucks in and out of a place under one of the chairs that he said was a parking lot at a diesel fuel station.

The minute he heard the orchestra start tuning up, he whispered, "Now it's time for us to start being quiet and put the trucks away."

When we were done with that, I picked him up and he snuggled back in my lap. "You're such a good boy, Parker," I said softly.

He looked up at me and put his finger to his lips. "Sh," he whispered. "We're not supposed to talk in concerts."

It was going to be the same program the orchestra had played in Edinburgh, all music by American composers: the *Adagio for Strings* by Barber, followed by Seneca playing *Rhapsody in Blue,* then Symphony no. 3 by a guy named Aaron Copland. I'd only heard parts of the symphony in the rehearsal in Scotland.

I suppose because she'd done such a great job playing in Edinburgh, I wasn't worried about how well Seneca would do that night, the way I had been at the Usher Hall. Still, I was anxious to have that first piece be over and hear her again.

Audiences always clap when the performer comes on stage, but when Seneca came out this time, they didn't just clap, some of them actually yelled, "Brava!" She bowed three times before they stopped applauding. She was wearing an electric-blue satin dress that shimmered as she moved and left her shoulders bare so you could see her wonderful muscles. It was a perfect color for her, and she looked great.

I remembered the first time I'd seen her perform. I thought of how scared she'd looked before she started to play. In Edinburgh I was pretty sure she hadn't looked scared anymore, but I hadn't noticed her expression much when she walked onto the stage.

This time I did. Obviously she always knew she could play the piano, but when she was up there in front of the crowd that night, she had a whole different kind of confidence. She stood up tall and straight, her head high in the air, and instead of looking scared, her eyes glowed. When she turned and sat down at the piano, she moved like a queen.

I think Seneca performed even better that night than she had in Edinburgh. She had such amazing energy! She seemed so strong as her hands came down on those keys in the pounding parts, so jazzy in the jazzy parts, so gentle in the soft parts. It was all just unbelievably good.

The audience jumped to their feet the minute she was finished playing, like they had at the Usher Hall, but this time there was a roar, with everybody shouting and clapping like crazy. The orchestra members who weren't holding instruments were clapping, and the string players tapped their bows on their music stands. Alexander Cameron kissed Seneca on both cheeks, took her hand and raised it into the air, and the roar got louder. Somebody handed her a bouquet. More kissing, more cheering.

The audience wouldn't let her leave the stage without playing not one, but two encores. I lost count of how many bows she took. Teresa's eyes were shining with tears as she left for her daughter's dressing room, but I thought they were tears of pride instead of sadness.

We didn't go backstage during intermission this time. I was kind of glad. It might have brought back too many bad memories. Instead we went out into the lobby and bought soft drinks for us and a cookie for Parker.

He was so cute in his white shirt and bow tie, and so incredibly sweet! I thought I loved him as much as I'd love a little brother, if I had one. I didn't even want to think about having to say good-bye.

Seneca and her mom waited until the lights went down for the second half of the concert before they came into our box, probably so that people wouldn't notice them. Seneca had changed into a cool white shirt and short black skirt that made her look very sophisticated. We all smiled at her and whispered congratulations and things while the conductor was coming out and taking his bow. She beamed back at us with that brilliant white smile of hers. Then the music started and we turned toward the stage.

I don't know if I'd ever heard Copland's Third Symphony before, but it instantly became one of my very favorite pieces of classical music. For the first minutes I just listened and watched the musicians. Then I happened to glance over at Seneca.

Even though I was enjoying the performance, I could see just from the way Seneca looked that she was into it in a whole different way. It was like the music was part of her. She knew every note, and she moved with it—not big movements, just little shifts in her shoulders, or raising her head and sitting up taller in some of the loud parts. Sometimes, when there was a really strong rhythm, it was like she had to hold herself back or her whole body would move.

She was all music. I remembered that moment in the boat when she told us about how she'd spent her time in the castle practicing piano in her head, and about coming across the moat on the rope humming and keeping time to "Scotland the Brave." I wondered if there was ever a day, or even a moment in her life, that music wasn't a part of, one way or the other.

Lucas and I had had a part in rescuing Seneca Crane from a lot of things. From Old Dalhousie Castle, from Green Socks and Mustache, from a stepfather and a tutor who were, as she had said, evil. And I thought that being with us had helped her make the final decision to take time off from her career.

But a lot of the changes in her were things that didn't have anything to do with us. I wondered if they had to do with God or fate or whatever. I remembered how she had seemed that first time we'd talked to her, at the McDonald's on Princes Street—half this really sophisticated concert performer, and half a little kid. I was pretty sure the little kid in her was gone forever now. And she wasn't timid like she had been when we first met her. She'd found out that on her own she could be brave and strong. When she escaped from the castle, she had brought Miss Bumble with her in the backpack. But I didn't think she'd need to sleep with her stuffed bunny anymore.

And Lucas and me—were we different because of what had happened to us in Scotland? I thought about being up there on that rampart in the storm, casting the fly line. It really hadn't occurred to me until that moment, but I realized that in the past weeks I'd also found out that I could be stronger and braver than I had ever thought possible.

I glanced at Lucas, who had a sound-asleep Parker in her lap. She'd met Jamie and discovered how wrong Josh Daniels was for her. And she'd found out what kind of a guy she was looking for.

A guy like that would come along sometime, maybe soon. And maybe there would be somebody for me. I hoped so. I kind of wanted to get into this Dance of Life thing.

But that was Garth Brooks. Tonight was Seneca's night, with Seneca's kind of music. I settled into my chair and turned back to the stage.

Acknowledgments

Putting this book together demanded an enormous amount of research, and helpful suggestions from what seems like an endless number of readers. In trying to give credit to all of the generous people who helped me along the way, I hardly know where to start.

Perhaps the best approach is to begin at the beginning, with my friend Gwen Pappas, director of public relations for the Minnesota Orchestra. Gwen took me backstage for an invaluable tour of the Usher Hall when the orchestra was appearing at the Edinburgh Festival. I must also thank the kind guards at the hall's stage entrance, who let me into the artiste's suite when I was in Edinburgh on a later trip. Thanks also to Kari Marshall, the orchestra's artistic administrator, for valuable information on artist contract technicalities.

No one on this list deserves more credit than Gillian Glenwright at the peaceful (and very highly rated, I might add) White Heather Hotel in Kyleakin, a lovely harbor town on the Isle of Skye. Gillian must be one of the friendliest, most generous and accommodating women on the planet. Long after I had been a guest in her hotel, she went to great trouble providing local color details and tracking down information. As if all this were not enough, she actually arranged a rescue of a camera I had accidentally left on my trip—in Inverness. What a woman! I cannot thank her enough.

A big thank you as well to Mike Alwin at Bob Mitchell's Fly Shop in Lake Elmo, Minnesota, for teaching me a lot about fly-fishing in a very brief period of time. And for not making me feel like an absolute idiot in the process. Equally helpful was Tammy McDiarmid, who provided a lesson in the tarot. I used her information and ran with it. In the case of these two recognized authorities especially, where there are errors in the book, they are mine, not theirs.

The Portree police answered a number of questions concerning policies and procedures. I am particularly grateful to Police Constable Paul Bennie—yes, there really is a Constable Bennie—who was extraordinarily friendly and helpful. And let me just give a shout out to all those nameless people at the other end of the phone at the Portree Tourist Information Centre who answered untold questions about the Isle of Skye, from shopping for outerwear on a Sunday morning in Portree to Scottish fly-fishing terminology. My friend Steve Smith, a.k.a., Dr. Stephen Smith, provided essential advice about medical issues.

So many people read this book and gave me great feedback that I fear I am going to forget at least one, and probably dozens. First off, I want to thank my young readers and consultants. Ellen Rethwisch and Ada Wolin read the manuscript through and provided terrific ideas. I acted on almost all their suggestions, and I am forever grateful to them. Lily Crutchfield, my authority on all things young and cool, helped me with terminology among the younger set. She would know.

Then there were the accents. My delightful friend Scotty Thomson provided perspective only available from an Edinburgh native. Ron Akehurst and Caroline Jewers had an eagle eye for dialect and language use throughout, and saved my bacon on a couple of important points.

All the members of the Crème de la Crime writers' group were helpful, as always. So a great big thank you to Anne Webb, Carl Brookins, Charlie Rethwisch, Jean Paul, Joan Loshek, Julie Fasciana, Kent Krueger, Michael Kac, Mary Monica Pulver, Scott Haartman, and Tim Springfield. Special thanks to those members who read the manuscript all the way through and gave me extremely valuable feedback, and to those who helped with the tricky ending. You know who you are. And special gratitude as well to Carl for assistance with all things nautical.

And to my family. Once again, Annalisa came through with wonderful comments on the manuscript. Her suggestions made the work stronger. And enormous thanks, as always, to Steve and Robyn and Rusty and Patty for many forms of input and assistance and consistent support.

And last but not least, thanks to my agent, Tina Wexler, and to Tracy Gates, my editor, and the highly professional team at Viking. You're awesome, you guys.

Good heavens—I hope that's everybody!

Susan Runholt shares a love of art, travel, and feminism with her teenage heroines, but maybe not their nerves of steel! After college, she traveled extensively in Europe and lived in Amsterdam and Paris, working as a bank clerk and an au pair. She's also been a waitress, a maid, a motel desk clerk, a laundress, a caterer, and eventually the director of programming for South Dakota Public Television. She now lives in Saint Paul, Minnesota, where she is a fundraising consultant for social service and arts organizations. Her first book about Kari and Lucas, *The Mystery of the Third Lucretia*, was named runner-up for the Debut Dagger Award by the Crime Writers' Association of Great Britain. You can learn more about Susan Runholt and her books at www.susanrunholt.com.